LUCY AT WAR

UNDRALAND
BOOK SEVEN

MARY E. TWOMEY

MARY E. TWOMEY, LLC

Lucy at War

Book Seven in the Undraland Series

By
Mary E. Twomey

COPYRIGHT

Copyright © 2015 Mary E. Twomey
Cover Art by Crowe Covers
Author Photo by Lisabeth Photography

For information:
http://www.maryetwomey.com

DEDICATION

For Madeline.
You give me courage when I can't find it,
and you find me when I'm not me.

To our many adventures.
May they always be filled with laughter,
long island iced teas,
And a little world domination.

CAPTURED

I awoke in the same cell I'd been held in for the past... I'm not sure how long. Suffice to say I'd been without a shower, the sun or sanity long enough to be on the edge of breaking down in horrifying tears on a daily basis. Though there were no windows, I was certain I was being watched by a dark blob above me in the corner of the ceiling. I saw it when the slot in the door opened to give me food. And by food, I mean tapioca-like oatmeal and water.

I moved my arms and fought back a groan at the heaviness of the iron shackles around my wrists. They'd trained me well in the time they'd held me in the concrete cage. If I made a noise, the hard collar around my neck sent a little shock through me. It was in proportion to the volume, so I made sure not to open my mouth at all. The old Foss would've been thrilled. The one I loved? I'd like to think he'd Hulk out and destroy everyone who'd imprisoned me, leaving any hint of diplomacy at home.

The sirens had poured something that burned like scalding honey down our throats when we'd first arrived at our lovely new abodes. It had damaged something in our throats, and I wasn't sure I wanted to think about the possible permanence of that. I guessed, though, that since they viewed the shock collar as a necessary tool to keep us quiet, that our throats would eventually heal.

I moved my arms again, shifting along the few inches I was allotted, pressing my lips together to silence the agony the slight jerk ripped through me. I was in the purest of blackness, unable to tell sometimes if my eyes were opened or closed. My arms were covered in a long-sleeved thin shirt and opera gloves to keep my painted stars from giving me any relief from the darkness. My wrists had been fitted with fetters – actual pirates or knights-era fetters, and the chains led to the floor, giving me precious little space to move at all. They didn't even allow me enough slack to stand, so I alternated between kneeling, sitting on my butt and lying down. I could do pushups, which I'd never been stellar at before, but as I had nothing else on my schedule, I kept myself motivated and focused by doing as many as I could before I collapsed. I'd worked my way up to twenty-five, which may not sound like a lot to you, but it was about four times more than I'd been able to do before my imprisonment. I was malnourished, so each one was an effort I didn't always have in me.

Tucker. Tucker will die for this. I'd never considered myself a violent person growing up, but that one mantra kept me going through each pushup, granting strength to areas I'd been weak in before.

Tucker St. James had been Jens's old friend on the Other Side, a fire elf who tricked us all into thinking he was helping to hide me and keep me safe. Boy, was I a lousy judge of character. I'd hugged him and let him hold my hand, giving him the benefit of the very legitimate doubt time and time again. I downgraded myself from nearly grown woman to utter flake. It was the naïve idiot in me who thought every monster was a kitten and every villain was misunderstood and redeemable. It was what had me voting against the death penalty growing up and pushed me towards Foss. In some ways, I won that bet on my former husband. He really had grown to be a little more considerate, tracking me down after searching across states for me. Of course, he'd unwittingly led a group of bounty hunters right to me, but it's the thought that counts. I wondered if Foss still thought of me as I did him.

Wherever he was, I was certain of one thing: Jens was searching for me, leaving only the rock I was under unturned. It was his stubbornness in conceding a fight that fed me spoonfuls of solace in my darkest of moments.

There had been thirty-two meals. I couldn't be sure if they were feeding me twice a day or once, but it was definitely not more than that. I did my best to keep track of the passing of time by the sliver of dimness that greeted me when a tray was pushed into the cell at just the right spot for me to reach it if I really stretched.

Jens would come for me. Jens was no doubt already on his way here, not that I knew where "here" was. Though, of the four men I'd ever kissed on the mouth, two were now dead. Best of luck for all involved.

I wondered where Jamie was, and knew they were giving him or me something to mute our bond. I could feel him in that fuzzy kind of way you can feel cold smoke, but can never really hold onto it. We kept slipping in and out of each other's minds, giving just enough human contact to keep me from turning into a raving maniac.

I was terrified, freezing and ached all over. The only bathroom privileges I'd been granted were in the form of a bucket with a lid just within reach of my tether. Though as they continued starving me, that need grew less and less. It was just as well; I hated that someone on the other end of that camera was watching me. A few times I gave them the finger while relieving myself. The next meals had been half-portions in punishments. While I wasn't above starving myself and rejecting any attempts at nourishment, I knew Jamie needed the sustenance. He had a baby on the way, and I wouldn't jeopardize him getting to have his dream for anything in the world. Someone would get something good in the end; I was determined. For the pacifist I used to fancy myself, I knew I would fight to the death for something that important. I needed Jamie to make it out of this. He'd been cursed enough of his life. I was determined not to add to his misery.

What bothered me, aside from the obvious, was that I had no idea why they were holding us. There had been no attempts to get information from me, no threats or demands made. I'd been simply fitted with the collar, given long-sleeved green scrubs to wear and cast into a pitch black cold cell that stank of freezing death.

Jamie? Jamie? Can you hear me? I called. I tried to check in with him periodically throughout the day, but the response was the same. I heard nothing. I felt the presence of my buddy, but couldn't get to him. It was unreal how much I'd grown to rely on our connection. Now that it was defunct in my hour of need, I had to fight with everything in me to stay calm. Jamie'd been the literal voice in my head to talk me out of ill-conceived ideas and coax me off a ledge. Now that he was muted, the loneliness and panic clawed at my insides, removing bits of flesh I desperately needed to keep from icing over.

My fingers were stiff as I curled them, hoping sensation would return soon. When people used the term "iron grip", they really had no clue. Though the irons didn't dig into my skin if I was careful and kept my fists straight, they allowed my wrists little movement and were heavy as all get-out.

Something invisible smacked me across the face, and I knew Jamie'd misbehaved. The surprise of it set loose a miniature squeak of pain, which sent a jolt of electricity through my body from my neck all the way to my toes. I silently sobbed and prayed that Jamie would stop, that he felt the sting on his end and realized I was barely holding on over here.

Jamie! Jamie, it's okay! You're alright, sweetheart. I'm here! I'll get us out of this somehow! Just stop pissing them off!

I tried my pep talk to myself that Jens would find us, that Foss would somehow best their top security, but it had been weeks. Though they were my own thoughts, I knew they were false hopes. No way would either of them let this go on as long as it had if they could rescue us. Either they were searching in the wrong place, or they had assumed us dead. I blinked my eyes a few times, willing tears to go away. The thought of Jens giving up on me sent a horror through my spine that made the cold feel like a joke.

Lucy? Lucy! I heard Jamie's faint cry in the foggy distance.

Jamie? I'm here! I can hear you! Trying to fend off my tears was no use at this point. Warm droplets heated my freezing face as they slid down my cheeks and splashed on the unmercifully hard floor.

It's the food! They're putting something in the food to numb the bond. Don't eat it! We'll die quicker if we don't have each other. Where are you? I can't see anything. I'm in a cell and have no clue where I am.

I was on my knees, leaning toward the door, pulling at my restraints. *I don't know where I am! I'm in the same kind of cell, but I haven't heard anyone outside of it. I don't know if it's soundproofed, or if we're just that far away from each other.* Quick as I could, I conjured up my living room in our shared imagination. As soon as the fireplace, leather sofa and clean olive walls - that were in all reality burned to a crisp - appeared, we ran to each other, attacking in hugs and kisses like frantic puppies eager to greet their best friend.

Jamie picked me up, and my legs wrapped around his waist. My thighs were strong again, not the weakened ones that were straining as I knelt on the concrete, blissed out in my vision. I cupped Jamie's bearded face and kissed it all over, sobbing as he did the same to me. Though we'd never been so affectionate with each other in real life, our desperation fueled us as we sought comfort in whatever manner possible.

Where are we? I'm so scared, Jamie! I'm losing my mind over here!

Me, too, syster. Me, too. His arms around me tightened as he collapsed backward onto the rich caramel-colored leather of the couch I'd spent days poring over catalogs to pick out. He positioned me so I was straddling his lap and continued kissing my face, and then his lips trailed down to kiss feeling into my arms. We were starved for physical touch. This kind of torture took its own awful toll. My proper prince was desperate, as was I. *Are you chained to the floor, too?*

Yes, and it's awful! If only they'd tell us what they want!

Jamie's voice was grave as he stopped kissing my arms

to look at me seriously. *No matter what, we must not give them anything. Do you understand me? If they ask your name, you don't tell them. Whatever they want, they won't get it.*

But, your baby! I protested. *We have to get you out so you can be there for your kid! I'll tell them anything to make that happen. We have to get you out of here!*

He shushed me and hugged my body, rubbing warmth into my cold places. *Jens will find us. All we have to do is stay quiet until then.*

I can't take much more of this! I cried, imaginary tears wetting his green scrub shirt. *Tucker stole my family's ashes! He took my necklace! I need them with me!*

My tears and our state of heightened anxiety brought about an admission of despair from Jamie. *They have rats in my cell. I hear them, but I don't see them, so I never know when it's safe to fall asleep without one of them gnawing on my face. It's unsettling.*

I combed my shaking fingers through his curly chestnut hair, shushing his increasing worry. *It's not real,* I told him, letting him in on a bit of technological torture I'd cottoned on to the first day. *It's just a recording made to make you think something creepy crawly's in your cell. Have you ever felt a rat brush up against you?*

No, he admitted. *You're certain? It sounds so real.*

Surround sound, baby. I held tight to him, our torsos pressed together. *So we're not eating?*

Not a bite, and don't drink the water either, he warned,

squeezing me so tight, I was grateful my need for air was only imaginary in our bond.

I could tell he wasn't going to hold up much longer under these circumstances, so I stated the obvious. *We won't last long without food or water.*

Jamie nodded, understanding the implications of our choice. *Then we die as ourselves, not the slobbering messes they intend on turning us into. We're not very much alive in here as it is.*

What about your baby?

Jamie clutched me and screamed into my shoulder. I held him as he let out the grief he was only just expressing. *They aren't going to let us go, Lucy. I don't know why they have us, but I gave up hope a month ago that they would turn us loose. My child will know I loved him or her through Jens and Britta telling them every day. Jens will care for my child as if it were his own. Jens will watch over Britta.*

He will, I agreed, swallowing through the agony of coming to terms with never seeing my perpetual dragon-slayer ever again. My brain caught onto something Jamie had said. *A month ago? I've counted thirty-two meals. Aren't they feeding us every day?*

No, honey. Thirty-two meals consisting of one cup of oats. I'm fairly certain they're feeding us once every other day. Two months. We've been here over two months. I think we've played their game long enough. I won't stay here another week.

I thought they were feeding us one or two times a day! There's no way we can survive on what they're feeding us! We'll die soon anyway! Even if the meals were calorie-fortified, which I had to guess they were, no one could live forever on gruel.

Jamie pulled back and nodded solemnly. *Then we make that choice. They don't decide when we die; we do.*

I returned his nod with tears, forming as much resolve as I could to resist the little food they gave us. I knew I'd thinned out by the looser fit of my filthy green scrubs, but as this was my imagination, I pictured myself as I wished I was – with a healthy amount of curves for a girl my age. I leaned my forehead against Jamie's and exhaled. *We live together or die together. Not another bite,* I agreed.

Jamie held me on his lap and brought my head to his shoulder to rest there. In our imaginations there were no rat noises, no torturous loneliness, and no social rules that kept men and women so very separate.

Jamie smiled into my hair. *I brought you something.* Into the living room scampered my gray squirrel. I'd conjured him up when Jamie'd needed a distraction to keep from losing his mind back when Jeneve poisoned him with a curse that twisted his gentle personality.

David Cassidy! I patted a spot on the couch next to us, and my sweet little squirrel jumped up so he could climb on our arms and perch on our heads and shoulders. *I forgot about this little guy. Hey, buddy!* I cooed, taking his bushy gray body into my hands. He pawed at Jamie's half-inch long beard, making us both laugh.

I hadn't laughed in what felt like ages.

Thanks, Jamie. I needed him. I tilted my head to the side as I examined my favorite prince. *You get me.*

I do. But then again, I have the owner's manual. Come here. Jamie pulled me into another hug, sighing contentedly as David Cassidy chittered between us. Though we were still freezing, the imagined body heat warmed our insides where it was needed most. *I love you, liten syster.*

I love you, I whispered. *Don't leave me alone in there. Two months!*

Never. I'll never leave you. He gripped me tighter. Though we were afraid, we would end this together.

LET IT COME

*W*hen the food tray came the next day, it was pushed through the small slot in the door just as it had been every other time. My stomach lurched while my body actually leaned to snatch at it.

Control! Jamie warned me. *We decide when we die!*

I let out a silent sob and shoved the tray out of reach. Now no matter how much I was tempted, my iron restraints wouldn't allow me to compromise the plan. Such a plan it was. Choosing to die.

I spent the next innumerable amount of hours saying goodbye to my parents, my brother, Tonya, Jens, Britta and Jamie. I couldn't think about Foss. I couldn't even conjure up his face or think his name – the pain was too great. I loved him too horribly to say goodbye to him. There was no part of me that would allow even his memory near my current state anymore. I was ashamed at how low I had come, and knew his disappointment in my bedraggled state would be the first thing he would comment on. I loved him, and I deserved to die with that self-inflicted burden.

Foss will always love you, Jamie told me, and I instantly wished for some of the bond-numbing food to keep my thoughts private. *No!* he scolded me. *I'll keep quiet, I promise. Don't eat the food!*

I just can't, I sobbed. *He's too... I'm too... I just can't. Don't say his name to me. I'm barely hanging on here.*

I'm here, Jamie assured me. My imagination was muted and bleak, so I could only conjure up an image of what I pictured I looked like in my cell, only with Jamie chained next to me, instead of wherever they had him holed up.

The rat noises multiplied, along with something squishy and creepy that kind of reminded me of a worm or a spider or something. My spine tingled, knowing they were amping up the fear factor due to our defiance.

My tears dried in that instant, and my besotted face drew into a menace I was glad I couldn't see in a mirror. *Let it come,* I thought as much to myself as to Jamie. *Whatever they've got for us? Let it come. I've got nothing left but breath, and I'll choose when that stops.*

That's my girl, Jamie growled with the same determined expression. Jamie leaned against me in my mind, in our respective cells. I sagged toward where I pictured him to be. We seethed in the dark for hours, waiting out our inevitable demise in silence.

3

—————

DEFIANCE

*T*he next day was the same. I had less strength with which to push my tray away, but when it slid out of reach, my anger at my invisible captors was renewed, even though it was with less energy to defy them.

I expected the rat noises that had kept us up and paranoid most of the night to increase in volume. What I did not expect was for them to cease altogether. The silence was a sigh of relief I wouldn't let them see I needed.

When a woman's voice cooed over the sound system, I cowered from the intrusive noise. "You should eat, children. You'll need your strength."

I wanted to answer back with the worst kind of bar swearing, but my collar had me trained to shut my mouth. Instead I gave her my favorite finger. The cuffs dug into my skin, cutting my bony wrists even through the gloves, so that every movement of my arms was a little bit painful.

It was worth it.

I sat on my knees as long as I could before that position grew too painful, and then shifted to sit on my butt, leaning back on my pained hands. Jamie did the same, nudging me with his shoulder in our bond. Though we were far away, we clung to the connection we'd both resented so many times.

No sooner had we shifted did our chains begin to clang on their own. They were attached to the floor, that much was obvious, but what was news to me was that the tether could be tightened or loosened by the powers that be. My little gesture of defiance earned us no slack at all. Our hands were sucked to the cold floor as the chain was fed through whatever reeled it in beneath the icy floor of the cell.

Jamie fought against the restraints, ripping our tender scrapes open, so blood seeped beneath the material of my gloves.

Stop! Stop, Jamie! I'm bleeding!

Jamie stilled with a defeated internal bleat of doom. *It won't be long now. Another couple days or so, and we'll pass on from this.*

My throat was parched, and I was running out of spit. My lips were dry and cracked, and I could only guess at the sad state the rest of me was in. We couldn't reach the toilet bucket, but that hardly mattered anymore.

MY INEVITABLE DEMISE

I had fallen into a fitful sleep that was only made worse by a nails on the chalkboard screeching. It played intermittently throughout our yanks from consciousness into passing out, and then back again. I could barely lift my head from my supine position when the door cracked open again and the tray was slid toward my foot. It smelled so heavenly, I instantly wondered if I was dreaming. It was beefy lasagna, the good and melty kind with what smelled like the right amount of too much cheese. My olfactory sense betrayed my resolve, and I made every effort to sit up to claw my way to the food, if only that were possible.

A clanking sounded, and suddenly too much slack was next to my hands. I slowly felt the chain and measured far more tether than we'd ever been granted.

No, Lucy! Stop! It's a trap! They'll cut me off from you, and it'll just be one more day they win! Don't touch the food!

I didn't want to go back on the plan, but I was less than half a human at this point, crazed from hunger and isolation. Every inch I earned toward my goal was an effort I didn't have in me to make. I crawled almost a foot before I collapsed, a besotted mess of crusted-over wounds, exhaustion and defeat. While I was certain I could reach the food with the additional tether they'd given me, my body rebelled against any effort. My heart still had a beat that I could feel, but it was the *only* thing I could feel, which wasn't a good sign. I was cold from the inside out, and the slowed and unsteady rhythm of my heart told me I didn't have much longer to wait out my inevitable demise.

It was then they did the cruelest thing I could think of. The cell went silent, and the chalkboard scratching noise was replaced with the sweetest voice I could've heard in that moment.

"Loos? I'll be home soon. Don't worry about a thing." It was Jens. My Jens.

Then came a shock through my collar. I didn't yelp, but my mouth opened in agony.

Did you speak? I asked, though I hadn't heard Jamie say anything. *Stop making noise, if you are!*

I'm not! I'm silent. Completely silent. Stay calm.

Jens's sweet voice sounded again. "I picked up the stuff to make dinner. That's right, baby, we're pretending we know how to cook tonight. How do you feel about crepes?"

Then he switched to a cartoonish French accent. "We could be French for the night. We should start with the French kissing. The crepes can wait."

Another shock jolted me, gritting my teeth without my permission. My jaw ached, and I could feel a ringing in my molars. I screamed in my mind, matching Jamie's inner noise of surprise and pain.

"I think we should take a trip to Paris. I've never been, and I want to see how our crepes match up to the real thing."

Another shock knocked me down so I was spread out on my stomach. I pictured Jens's face, but after three more playbacks of his voice followed by shocks, I couldn't see him without feeling the hesitance of fear his face was now associated with.

Part of me knew it was a recording they'd kifed from my voicemail to urge me onward toward living and enduring more of their psychological torture, but the less rational part of me rallied at the sound of my boyfriend's voice. I wanted out. They would not ruin my memories of Jens. I would find them – whoever they were – and tear them apart. For that, I needed sustenance.

With shaking fingers, I tried to support my dwindled weight and pull myself forward towards the food, but try as I might, I couldn't move myself. Jamie screamed his tired warning in my head to stop me, but it was an unnecessary effort. I was going to die; that choice had been made, and there was no going back.

I love you, Jens, I thought to the universe before my head rested on the concrete. It was as good a place as any to breathe my last. At least Jens hadn't had to watch my ending. When it came down the grit of it, he'd been with me, keeping me sane all the way up until the last when they tried to shock his comfort out of me. Jens was a good man, and I hoped he'd find peace without Jamie and me around to center his brash tendencies.

I closed my eyes, feeling Jamie lie down beside me in my mind, weakened and worn. He placed his hand atop mine so we wouldn't be alone as we died. He had more bulk to lose, so his body kept me just barely alive, but my meager weight pulled him down further. We were huddled together until I drifted off into a land where I couldn't control my imagination anymore. I couldn't control anything.

THE KINDNESS OF STRANGERS

ater poured over my face and splashed into my mouth. I swallowed reflexively, but the effort cost me great pains to get that mouthful down. I shuddered at the splash into my empty stomach. A warm body held me, and without making the conscious choice, I burrowed into the heat, convulsing as I was reminded of how freezing my skin was in comparison.

"That's good. Keep drinking. Little sips, or it'll come right back up." The voice was a man's, but I'd never heard it before.

I was soaking wet and ice cold, so when I shivered, it racked my body so hard, my ribs ached from the violent spasms. The low male voice instructing me was patient and sincere, so the emaciated and highly suggestible girl I was when on the brink of death wanted to trust him.

The Jamie inside of me was shouting, *No! No, Lucy! They'll sever the bond again! Spit it out! We were so close!*

We had been close. Close to death. In fact, I wasn't entirely sure how alive I actually was. I couldn't see anything, but I was certain I didn't know the man that held my limp form in one burly arm that had coarse hair I could feel through my wet scrubs. His other hand fed me small portions of water.

"Get me a blanket in here!" he shouted, his tone turning sharp like a militaristic command. After a brief pause, he barked, "I don't care what your reasons are. I don't care about your plan! You'll kill her before it works!" Another pause, and then he seethed, "You had your turn, and now you're done. This whole experiment failed. *You* failed. Look what you've done to her!" I guessed he was talking into an earpiece or Bluetooth or something, because I couldn't hear the person on the other end.

The man who held me sounded genuinely concerned, so I knew it had to be a trap. I used what little strength I had ("strength". What a joke) to squirm away from him. It didn't actually work, but the message was clear. "Now, now. I won't hurt you. I shouldn't have let them carry on without my supervision. I thought they understood the goal, but I was wrong. I'm sorry, sweet girl. I won't hurt you."

The man spoke so softly; every word was like a massage to my deadened muscles and broken heart.

No, Lucy! It's a trap! Don't believe a word he says! He's with them!

I could still hear Jamie, though I'd drank a fair amount of water, so I gathered at least the water was safe and wouldn't take Jamie away from me. Once my throat got used to the motion of swallowing, I leaned my chin toward the cup, begging silently for more.

"That's a good girl," he cooed, talking to me as if I was a cherished pet instead of an adult with a little dignity. In all actuality, I really had no pride left to hold onto, but he could've at least pretended in an effort to be nice.

He kissed my oily forehead, and I nearly sobbed aloud at the humanizing contact. I didn't made a sound, though, as I was afraid of triggering my collar and sending a shock through my body that would certainly kill me. "It's okay. I'll make sure this ends." Then to his earpiece, he barked, "Where's that blanket?" He was alternately kind and harsh, which jerked my emotions around as to whether I could allow myself to feel safe with him.

Think about it, Lucy! Of course they'd send a big, gentle man of authority to coerce you into whatever it is they want you to do. You'll notice they didn't send you a woman. It's part of the game! They want you to trust him. Hold strong, syster!

Jamie had so much more clarity than I did. I marveled at his strength of purpose. I was amazed by his tenacity to defy the powers that be.

I was amazed, and then I was unconscious, passed right the smack out in the cell. The man's pleas for me to wake up drifted in and out like waves on a beach.

SIX

I awoke to the same cell I was certain I would die in any time now. My eyes opened to the darkness, but something odd hit me. The air wasn't the bone-chilling cold it had been, but was an almost pleasantly warm temperature. I tried to sit up, but my body was too weak to commit to the effort, so I simply remained supine on the... blanket? The empty cell had grown a blanket since I'd last greeted it. The thick comforter underneath me offered a cradling to my aching bones, easing the joint pain that came with starvation and dehydration.

I moved my left arm and felt the brush of a second blanket draped atop me. I also felt the bliss of nothing. The irons were gone, and I could move. Theoretically, at least. I was too wasted away to actually put my muscles to use, but the tease of freedom rallied me enough to be able to open my eyes and actually focus on my surroundings.

The illumination, I realized, came from me. My arms had been uncovered. The stars glistened in the dark, giving just enough light to scare me into shutting my eyes. It was more comfortable to revert back to the stark nothingness I'd grown conditioned to. It took a few more seconds of psyching myself up before I tried opening my eyes again. I could make out a vague shape, whereas there had only been a black abyss for months. As my eyes put themselves to use, I realized the shape was a man that was certainly not Jamie.

My intake of breath alerted the stranger that I was awake and aware enough to know I wasn't alone. I tried to retreat from his advance, but I couldn't get my body to cooperate. He raised his hands in surrender and slowed them, but I panicked all the same, clawing futilely at the blanket.

"It's alright, Lucinda. I won't hurt you. Calm down."

No one called me by my actual name. The last time I'd been full-named was when I'd done Linus's take-home English Lit exam in high school and turned it in as his when he was in the hospital. My mom was not pleased. My dad kinda was, but he never admitted to it. But this guy didn't know me, and I certainly didn't know him. When he reached for me, my mouth opened in a silent scream.

"Shh. It's okay. I told you no one would hurt you anymore. I'm a man of my word." His arm went around my back and lifted me to sitting, cradling me against him again. The comfort was there, but so was the fear. It didn't matter, though, because I couldn't fight against him. He gathered the blankets up with me and lifted me up off the ground like a limp noodle, making his way to the door. It opened so easily for him. The steel barrier I'd been willing for months to budge to no avail popped open with a nudge from his knee.

The light hit me like the blinding sun, though I knew it was just a single bulb my eyes warred with. I bucked lamely in his arms, turning my face into his chest to block out the light.

"Oh, my mistake. I'm sorry." He brought the top blanket up over my head, and I relaxed, floating wherever he decided to take me. "Is that better?" I nodded in response, and he gave me a gentle squeeze. "It'll take time to adjust."

He greeted a few passersby, one who asked curiously what he had in the blankets. "It's the girl," he answered, as if my gender identified all that I was.

His brief reply earned a few gasps, a couple hisses and one "Get that thing out of here!"

He clutched me closer, as if to shield me from the insult. I had to remind myself that I was a prisoner, and he was part of that system, no matter how nice he was being in this particular moment.

I was carried to an unlit bedroom with no windows and laid atop the mattress. The luxury felt heavenly until the stranger sat on the side of the bed, reminding me that I was alone with a man and had no way to defend myself.

My breathing grew shallow as flashes of the Nøkkendalig rammed themselves into my brain. Before I knew it, I was hyperventilating, my aching ribs protesting the workout I gave them with my fear.

His arms were back around me, sitting me up and making a show of breathing slowly as he took in my face. "It's alright. You don't have to be afraid. No one's going to hurt you here. I'll turn on the lights once your eyes can handle them."

The blanket fell from my face, revealing a dark bedroom with the door opened just enough to allow the most light I could handle to filter in and give shape to the objects surrounding me. I winced from the light, but was able to squint with some success after a few tries.

Wooden nightstand built into the wooden wall. Lush comforter on a modern bed with no footboard that was also built to jut out from the wall. A chair in the corner pushed up to a desk that was attached to the wall. The room was a space-efficient cube with no clutter whatsoever.

Most jarring of all was the face that spoke to me. I didn't know his brown eyes, tightly pressed lips or thick black hair with gray at the temples, but I understood compassion when it was staring me in the face. His angular jawline and high cheekbones were set in determination that I would understand his role in all of this was one of safety, not aggression. I took a leap and trusted him for the time being. It wasn't as if I had much of a choice anyway. He'd gotten me out of the cell, so that was a point in his favor.

I leaned forward into his shoulder, and he melted into me, rubbing my back and holding me upright in his arms. "That's the way. One step at a time." I silently sobbed into his... uniform? He was wearing something like a cross between one of those harsh button-downs police officers wore and a t-shirt. I couldn't figure it out by touch alone. His voice was kind. "You're a tough one. I can't believe you lasted as long as you did. I can't believe they took it as far as they did, and they still lost." He touched his ear and spoke to whoever was on the other end of his little earbud intercom. "The female needs something to eat. Bring her up some bread and beans."

His words didn't explain as much as I needed, but it mattered little; I was so distraught. Once I had my wits about me, I would demand names and vengeance. For now, he offered comfort, so I took it.

He stroked my spine and spoke to me in a soothing lull that chased away a small amount of panic. "Food's on its way. Real food, and not the gruel you've been barely surviving on. You shouldn't be mad at them; they were trying to help."

I didn't speak, for fear the only thing that would birth from my mouth would be a voracious growl that would send more lightning through me via my collar. I shifted my neck and realized with astonishment that my stiff collar was gone! It took a bit of effort, but eventually my hands verified that my neck was bare. Though I had no desire or ability to speak, just knowing a punishment wasn't awaiting me alleviated my anxiety by a noticeable degree. When the food came up a few minutes later, my shoulders were almost ready to relinquish their death grip on me.

My stomach nearly exploded out of my body to get at the food, but my arms were still slow to cooperate. The guy holding me tore off fingerfuls of the warm bread and fed them to me, his thumb stroking my cheek every now and then as I chewed. He fed me slowly so my body didn't reject the foreign element it needed, but still feared. The starving amoebas in my belly jumped like a mosh pit inside of me, gobbling up and savoring each bite I could choke down. He alternated every three bites of bread with a sip of water, balancing the nurturing with great care.

When the bread was gone, I cried soundlessly into his shirt, daring to trust in the hope that came with his kindness. I couldn't hear Jamie, so I knew the food was tainted, but I was beyond caring at that point. I yearned for my friend, my one touchstone in the sea of never-ending crazy. They'd stolen my moxie, and in turn, robbed me of myself. I sobbed tearless cries of the agony I was sure would never leave me. The darkness would be my one faithful friend, the isolation a fixed weight on my innards.

Jamie? I called, aching for my friend. I'd caved and denied our purpose. I'd given in and let the enemy decide the rest of my life for me. I deserved the silence that greeted me, though I knew it wasn't on purpose. The bond was muted, and I felt hollow, a gnawing ache that ate at what was left of my stomach lining.

The man tipped a cup to my lips, giving me small swallows one at a time so my stomach didn't reject the little it had to work with. He was tender, and I was beyond vulnerable. I was pathetic, and I hated myself for it. He seemed to understand and kissed my forehead with his mustached lips, which was no longer quite so oily. I glanced down and noticed for the first time that I was wearing different clothes. It was a tribute to my besotted state that it had taken me this long to notice. That, and the dim light provided by my arms didn't give a ton of clues as to the details of my new life in captivity. I was wearing new green hospital scrubs. I shifted and realized I was wearing new underwear and had been bathed while I was out. Panic gripped me again at strangers deciding things for my body I'd not given them permission to.

The man lowered me down gently as if he completely understood my anxiety, though I knew I hadn't spoken a word. "I had a female nurse bathe and dress you. You're safe, now that I'm here. Nothing bad will happen to you while I'm around." He leaned over me and kissed my forehead again, adding a fair amount of pressure to center my spluttering brain. He smelled of a mountain-like manly body wash. I exhaled into his clavicle, permitting myself to believe him, even if it was a lie. It was a beautiful lie, so I clung to it as truth, holding it in my heart so I didn't drift away.

The older man pulled away and sat up beside my limp legs on the bed, angling his body so he was looking down on me and had full access to touch my face. Everything was confusing, but that was the most unsettling. I didn't like strangers touching my face – that much I knew. At the risk of earning the wrath of the only person who'd been good to me, I turned my cheek away from his soft caress, making my preference clear.

His hand froze, and then retracted in apology. "I'm sorry. You're right, you don't know me. I'm Captain Six, short for Sixten. I knew your mother a very long time ago. Long before she crossed over to the Other Side, which is where you are now."

I'd suspected as much, but it was nice to have the world I was in confirmed. I turned my face to look at him in the dim illumination cast by my arms. I had to squint so my eyes didn't wuss out on me, but it was good enough. Six was older, perhaps fifty, with thick black hair that had wisps of gray tickling his sideburns and a trimmed mustache. He was sort of handsome in that way adult women swoon over George Clooney, and the uniform bridged any gap to complete the picture of authority. He had kind brown eyes beneath salt and pepper eyebrows, but I could tell he knew how to erase the sweetness on a dime when needed. He was tall, like a true Undran, and his bulk was somewhere between Jamie's and Jens's.

When I said nothing, he continued to fill the silence he

assumed was uncomfortable for me. "You're undergoing treatment."

Treatment? Treatment for what?

My eyebrows must've said as much, because Captain Six answered me. "They took extreme measures with you. To be honest, we've never attempted to sever the bond, so we're a little out of our league. But not to worry, we'll find a way to break it. We just need more time."

Break it? Break the bond? Like, the laplanding link to Jamie? Where was Jamie? I shook my head and tried tapping my temple to communicate I couldn't reach Jamie, but all I managed to do was poke myself in the jaw.

The captain misunderstood and assumed I wanted more food, which I actually did. He brought the tray to the bed and sat beside me, his back against the wall as he brought me into his arms again to prop me up. I hated that I had to trust him. I despised myself for letting him feed me small bits of a banana that would undoubtedly keep Jamie from me. What were they doing to him while I was being cared for? I knew he was still there, but I was met with a fuzzy fog that kept me from him whenever I tried reaching out.

When I finished the last of the banana and a few more swallows of water, I could feel small amounts of lucidity creeping back to me, though I dared not act on any of it. The desk in the corner had papers on it, but I wouldn't go near it even if I could. I didn't want to be thrown back into that cell. I would be the best prisoner they had ever seen and cause no problems. I would be silent, since it seemed that was what they liked. I would eat when they fed me and blink when they told me.

My arms glittered, despite the lack of an overhead light to reflect off of. I was my own light, and now that Captain Six was here, they wouldn't take that away from me anymore.

A knock sounded at the door, so Captain Six laid me back down on the bed and left the room to speak with the person. I heard an angry exchange I couldn't decipher, followed by the captain coming back to my bedside with a clipped, yet apologetic tone. "We're moving you. Part of your treatment. Our facility has to remain hidden, so much that the infrastructure needs to stay a mystery to outsiders, which, I'm afraid you are." He lifted my hand and leaned over me to press my limp fingers to his chest. "I know it's not ideal, but we have to sedate you to move you."

Right on cue, a man in blue hospital scrubs wheeled in a cart with tubes and syringes on it. Even in the barely there light, I saw enough details to give full birth to a level of panic I didn't know I could reach. I shook my head and burrowed away from the captain, edging my uncooperative body toward the opposite side of the bed. Eyes wide with terror, I pushed myself off the bed, landing with a thud on a concrete floor. My bleat of agony was silent. They'd trained me so well with that cursed shock collar that I was afraid to make a noise. My wrist cracked horribly when I tried to push myself off the floor. My legs weren't working

– a product of not being able to walk or even stand for months on end. I tried to army crawl away, but knew it was futile.

Captain Six picked me up like the useless ragdoll I was and kissed my cheek, his mustache prickling my skin. His voice was like a tender lover's as he cooed softly to me, "You shouldn't run from me, Hildy. I can take care of you this time. Rolf got you killed, but I could've saved you. I can still save you."

My stomach churned, instantly ill at the old man looking at me with Romeo eyes. Horror gripped me when he called me my mother's nickname. I tried to twist away from him, but it was no use. Bile rose up in me at the sickness I could now see in Six's kindness.

The male nurse in blue hospital scrubs jabbed a needle in my arm, and my body started to go limp. I was at the mercy of a sad man who was in love with my mother. There would be no peace in the darkness that took me under once again.

7

TRYING

The darkness of the medicine-induced slumber lasted longer than my normal fitful sleeps. I used the opportunity to make a mad dash to Jamie as soon as I reached a solid REM cycle. In my dream, I was fast. I ran like an Olympian and never grew tired of the freedom that came with the ability to use my legs for all they were worth. I called out to Jamie as loud as I could down the hallway that our brains shared. There were no collars here, nothing to shock me into silence.

It took a solid minute of searching, but when the sight of his face reached me, I started sobbing without shame. We ran toward each other, and just before I crashed into him, I jumped up and landed in his arms. My legs wrapped around his waist as I clutched my friend, my one touchstone in this soulless place. *Jamie! Jamie! Where have you been?*

Where have you *been?* he asked, tears falling down his cheeks and running into his thickening beard. *I told you not to eat the food! It cuts us off from each other. Never again, Lucy! I can't hold on much longer! I'm losing my mind in this cell!*

You're still in your cell? I inhaled the scent of him. Though it was all memory and dream, I conjured up the oatmeal cookie smell I always associated with Jamie. I kissed his cheek over and over, burying my lips in the softness of his chestnut beard. *Jamie, where are you? You can't be far if I don't have a headache.*

I haven't moved! I'm wasting away slowly in the same spot I've been since I got here. You're out? How? Did you escape?

No! I responded mournfully. *This man, Captain Sixten, got me out. He seemed okay at first. Fed me, took me to a room with a bed. But then...*

Jamie jumped to the wrong conclusion, his face draining of color. *No! No, Lucy! He didn't touch you, did he? Damn these chains!*

I shushed Jamie, trying to exercise a level of calm I didn't totally feel. I ran my fingers through his hair that our imaginations had made clean and devoid of grease. *He didn't do anything like that. But Jamie, he's off. He called me Hildy, which was my mother's nickname. He knew her, and either he keeps getting confused and thinks I am her, or he wants me to be the her that left him or whatever. It's real messed up, and I'm afraid to wake up. But no, he hasn't done anything gross. I can barely move, and they knocked me out to move me around to a new room.*

Jamie bellowed his frustration into my hair. *We have to get out of here! What haven't we tried?* Jamie stilled, his death grip on my ribs loosening. *Wait, did you say you're out of your chains?*

I nodded. *But I'm too weak to move.*

Porting! Jamie said, his angst shifting to Christmas-morning level of excitement. *You're an elf, so you can port! The irons prohibit porting. That's why the jail cell in Elvage was made of iron. But your irons are off now? Do it! Port your-self to my cell, and then yank us out.*

What little hope there was in my face fell at his sugges-tion. *Jamie, I don't know how to do that. I can't port. No one's ever even tried to teach me. Besides, wouldn't I have to know where I'm porting to? Like, be able to visualize it at least? I have no clue where you are.*

Jamie dropped me so I stood in front of him, his face angry at what he assumed was laziness. *You have to try, Lucy! You can't just give up like that. It's our only hope. Our only way out of here.*

But it's not a real way! It'd be just as easy for you to port us out of here. I have way less magical experience than I'd need to do something like that. Be reasonable, Jamie! I've never done even the simplest magic!

No, you need to stop being reasonable! The old Lucy wouldn't just give up. She'd find a way! Jens called you Moxie. This isn't you! He shook my shoulders until my teeth rattled. *What are they doing to you?*

I don't know! I sobbed. I was a pathetic mess, and the

angry look in his eyes told me just how ashamed he was at my defeat.

I won't comfort you if you're not going to even try. I won't hold you while we slowly die anymore. If you want to talk to me, don't come back until you have a plan.

Then Jamie did the most horrible thing he'd ever done to me. My big brother turned from me and walked away.

Stop! Wait! Jamie, no! Please don't go! Please don't leave me! I need you! When he didn't turn back to me, I shouted, *I don't know how to fix this! I'm not Alrik!*

Then a thought occurred to me. It was so simple, I instantly felt stupid for having pushed it aside. I wasn't just Alrik's daughter. I was my father's daughter. My dad was a wind elf. Though I didn't have even the basics down for holding onto my magic, wind could be a useful tool if I could learn to harness it.

My shoulders sank. I couldn't command anything. I couldn't even stand. *Jamie?* I called. Though he didn't answer, I knew he could hear me. *I think I need your help.*

8

<hr>

USELESS DOMSLUT

amie was a thorough teacher, for someone who didn't possess elfin magic. The iron on my wrists had kept me from practicing, but Captain Six had removed my shackles from me. I was ruled harmless, which was a slam all on its own.

I awoke after a lengthy lesson in magic with Jamie, finding myself in a room no bigger than Six's. It was a square space with a single cot, and a desk in the corner. It seemed like a template they must've copied from room to room.

They?

Finding out who had their hooks in me was job one. Getting out was job two. My homework from Jamie was to use my newfound freedom to build up my muscles again. I could barely sit up against the wall that served as a headboard. My legs were useless, but I tried not to focus on that. I wished that my wind control was such that I could whoosh myself up to standing, but part of me knew that wasn't within the realm of possibility.

Don't get ahead of yourself. You still have yet to show any aptitude with wind. Jamie and I had been at this all night and day, clinging to our connection lest it be taken away. *Try it again.*

I blew on my fingertips as Tucker had done when he tried to get me to locate my magic. He'd used the brief window that I accepted tutelage from him to make pervy comments, which gave me yet another reason to hate him. *When we get out, we show no mercy for Tucker. Kill first, explain to Jens later.* Jamie and I both winced at mention of Jens. We'd been shocked so many times while hearing his voice. The pain associated with his memory became engrained, and completely unfair.

Focus, Lucy! Follow the heat.

Right, sorry. I breathed again onto my fingers that were pressed in supplication in front of my chest. Heat was a difficult thing to feel, but I did my best to catch onto the thread and trace it through my body. I made it all the way to my elbows before I lost it. *I'm getting better.*

Still not close enough, though. You haven't been able to follow the power down to your stomach, which is where your magic is held. I need you to concentrate harder.

Really? You want that? How about I turn off the TV first

and put away the popcorn. You want me to concentrate? Oh! You should've said so in the first place. Captain Six had fed me four simple meals in the past two days. I was regaining a little of myself with every bite. This was unfortunate for Jamie, who received the brunt of my frustration in the form of sarcasm.

Jamie was patient, biding his time through my fit. *Are you quite finished?*

I huffed, pressing my palms together. I was grateful the captain left me alone for large stints during the day. It gave me a lot of time to practice. Not that trying over and over to get past my elbows did a darned thing. My eyes squinched shut, my dry lips pursed together and I willed all that I was into the heat. It felt like a vine inside of me, but it was slippery somehow, and hard to hold onto.

After two more hours of this, I admitted defeat. *It's no use. Something's blocking me from bridging that connection. I don't get it. Maybe too many magics in me caused a short?*

Jamie's tone was kind, albeit bored. *You're not short. You just feel that way compared to all of us. I've seen enough of your kind to know you fall somewhere in the middle.*

I smiled. *I meant something else, but thank you. I guess Tor was right when he said halfies weren't as useful. Muddied genetic pool or something.*

Jamie laid down on the carpeted floor of my psyche, no doubt tired of watching nothing happen all day long. *I've never known a h-halfy to have a firm grasp on their magic,* he admitted, clearing his throat over his unexpected stutter. *I just thought if anyone could break the mold, it would be you.* He preferred hanging out in my brain to escape his, and I welcomed the company now that Captain Six saw to them not poisoning us anymore. The situation was still dire, but it was a wonder what a little food did to a person's mood.

Thanks, big brother. The thing about a good brother is that they know when to push you and when to back off. I'd had Linus, who'd been a pro at that, and now Jamie. A girl would be lucky to have one brother in her life, but now I had two.

Jamie picked a few errant thoughts from my mind, returning my smile. *I love you, too. I never loved my own sister as much as I care for you, nor have I felt love from her as I feel your affection for me.*

You're just saying that because she tried to kill you, I joked glibly.

Captain Six entered the bedroom I was being held in, interrupting and evaporating my time with Jamie. As usual, I scooted as far away from him as I could, regarding him with wary eyes and distrustful body language. Though I couldn't speak, I wanted the "stay away" vibe to ring out like a gong. Lucy Kincaid would not play nice with strange men.

The captain set down a tray on the nightstand, looking over at me with a hopeful smile I suppose had a touch of warmth to it. "Good morning," he breathed, looking at me as if I was the Holy Grail. "I brought you some fruit. Do you think you could try a few bites?"

I blinked at him, unwilling to answer, lest he think we were friends and I trusted him. To be fair, I had a small fraction of trust for Captain Six only in the sense that I ate the food he brought me. It hadn't taken Jamie away from my mind, so I trusted him only inasmuch as him not tainting my food, and my biological imperative to eat.

The captain set the tray between us, offering the food without feeding it to me. Since I'd regained basic motor function in my arms, I didn't require assistance. He'd learned from our last meal not to try that nonsense again. He'd tried to put a piece of a roll in my mouth. It was promptly spat out and the tray knocked over. I knew I risked my privileges being taken away, but I had standards. I wasn't going to be his pet or his girlfriend or whatever this was. He'd cottoned on to the rules and adhered to them for the most part.

He still called me Hildy. Ain't no shrink qualified enough to wade through that.

"I thought you might want to have breakfast with me in the cafeteria," he said, making sure to keep his voice soft so as not to invoke the crazy in me that was too near the surface. He leaned down and whispered, "If you're very good, they're going to let me keep you."

I shuddered and screamed in my mind.

"Once you're better, you'll stay here with me."

I didn't know what to make of his offer, but as it turned out, it wasn't actually a request. He rolled in a wheelchair and lifted me off the bed as if I was made of brittle bone and silk. I could sit up well enough on my own to where I didn't require the straps to hold me upright in the wheelchair. When he bent down on one knee to place my feet on the narrow platform, he paused, steeling himself before pressing his lips to my knee.

Jamie roared in my head as my mouth dropped open in a silent scream. I raked my clumsy and malnourished nails across his cheek, barely leaving a mark, since I'd taken to excessively biting my nails. Though I didn't hurt him, my intention was clear.

With sad eyes that pitied me, he held my hands while still on bended knee. "Hildy, don't do that. You love me. I knew you'd find us. I knew you would come back to me."

I struggled to free myself from the chair and him. I didn't care how I escaped – I'd crawl along on my elbows if that's what it took. Though I hadn't uttered a word, Captain Six seemed to understand enough of my disgust towards him that he pulled back, though he still held my hands.

"They all think we're dead. They think they killed us all, but you can't vanquish an entire race this superior!" The gleam in his brown eyes bordered on madness. "Our siren abilities don't work on the Other Side. The moment we fled through the gates, they were stripped away. You notice my hair? It's not the silver it used to be, coated in stars. Once we crossed over, we became common. We can't burn with our hands anymore, and our skin that used to be translucent clouded over to look like humans." He unloaded the information with a heavy sigh, conveying his disappointment. "Tucker St. James built us a bunker, and we've been down here ever since. A few try living under your sun, but most live down here. Did you figure that out, too? Did you find some way to restore our power to us, Hildy? If anyone could do it, it'd be you. This is all that's left of our people. Please tell me you can help."

He looked up at me with such sincerity and hopefulness, I almost pitied him as I shook my head. His shoulders sank, and he buried his forehead in my lap.

However many sirens were down here were impotent. That was good to know. I'd thought Pesta was the big kahuna, but apparently the mole people down here were still holding on. To know such power only to have it stripped away just because you stepped over to the Other Side was harsh.

Jamie raged in my head. *Don't you dare soften, Lucy! He's part of this! He's part of why we're being held down here!*

I know! I'm just saying it sucks, is all. Impressive they built this underground area to survive in.

Survive? You mean to torture people in!

I know, I know. Chill out.

Captain Six stood, leaning over me to kiss my forehead. I cringed at the mustache I now hated, and thankfully he pulled back. "They say they've got more work to do to try severing the bond before I can keep you." He traced the curve of my cheek, so I ripped my face from his touch. "Don't you want to be free of that Tonttu brat?"

My nose scrunched as I touched my heart with a feeble and shaking hand, indicating that Jamie was dear to me.

Six nodded, now pitying me. "Yes, you may feel that way now, but his father was one of those who ordered our banishment. Our land was taken and redistributed among Undra. They grow their crops on stolen land!"

His scandalous announcement was, I'm sure, upsetting. I, however, had been shocked around the neck too many times to feel terribly bad for anyone except for Jamie and me.

I saw the consequence of breaking the bond, clear as day. If they were successful in severing the lapland, Jamie would be unprotected. In this place, he wouldn't last a day with the amount of jaded sirens holed up for two decades in here. I reached through the bond and clung tight to Jamie's hand. *I won't leave you. No matter what.*

Jamie squeezed my hand in response just as Six laced his fingers through mine. I held tight, meaning to attach myself to Jamie, but Six benefitted from my small compliance. "That's right. You're starting to remember me. I know it's been years. Your daughter doesn't like me much."

My nose scrunched again. I didn't have the psych degree necessary to deal with his level of Looney Tunes.

I yanked my hand from his, but he smiled, walking around behind my wheelchair and pushing me through the dark toward a cafeteria area. "I had them turn off the lights so you don't hurt your eyes," the captain explained, leaning over my shoulder to speak quietly to me. No one was in the hallway except for us, though I could hear people moving through other nearby hallways.

One short-haired middle-aged woman in blue scrubs turned down our hallway, saw my arms and gasped, shrieking in accusation at me. "*Domslut*! She should die, Captain! All due respect, but it's an insult to have a *Domslut* in our home! She killed one of us and wears our blood like a medal of honor!"

Captain Six ran his fingers through my hair. I jerked my chin toward the floor so I didn't have to see her hatred or feel his affection. "Anika, Lucinda's of no harm to us. She did what they told her to do. This is Hilda the Powerful's daughter. She won't hurt us now that Undraland isn't pulling the strings. Once we separate her from the Tomten who's brainwashed her, I'm sure she'll be more than helpful with our situation."

Jamie scoffed in my head.

Anika was not pacified. "We're fine without her. She spilled siren blood. I want hers in return!" As she walked by us, she spat at me, the wet gob landing in my hair. "Dom*slut*," she seethed, emphasizing the part that played best to her vindictive nature.

Sure. Now I'm a slut. Whatever.

Captain Six wasted no time in retaliating. He pulled a small whistle from under his shirt and blew on it four times in succinct blasts. He grabbed Anika and slammed her to the wall in front of me. He cupped her chin with his unforgiving hand and forced her to look at me. His words were squeezed out through clenched teeth. "That is Hilda the Powerful trapped inside her daughter's body. Hilda fought for our freedom before she was banished, as we are. You'll not assault her in my presence." Though he'd been kissing my fingers minutes before, he was brutal now, and I was very afraid.

Anika gave a few attempts at breaking free, but then deflated. "Yes, Captain."

Three orderlies wearing more official-looking shirts than the average torturer or resident ran in from other hallways. It was enough commotion that I was ignored for the moment. I had very little use of my legs, but my arms were regaining motion. I took my chance as Anika yelled her accusations at Six and flung my body forward out of the wheelchair. Jamie cried out in my mind, but the pain was quickly replaced with cheers for me to go faster, to escape. There was no plan, only away, so away I crawled, using my forearms as leverage to slink a foot at a time away from the madness.

Anika was led away after Six explained the charge. Apparently it was fine to starve me, shock me, and keep me locked up in darkness, but Heaven forbid anyone spit at me. I didn't understand their moral compass, but I was grateful for this one finally swinging in my favor.

My victory was short-lived, if you can believe it, solid as my plan was. Six picked me up like I weighed nothing and set me back in the wheelchair. "You shouldn't have done that! I was getting you cafeteria privileges. Hildy, I know you're in there! Control your daughter!"

Instead of trusting me to stay in the chair, he pulled the straps that had been hanging on the arms and fastened them too tight for comfort. He turned the wheelchair around and steered me straight back to the room I'd been granted, shutting the door behind us.

9

KUNNA TOFS

My arms lit the room, and I was grateful he didn't try to turn on any additional lights. The brightness from just the stars was too much still.

I thrashed against my bindings, panicking that I was in a room alone with the crazy man. He looked me over, calculating how best to approach the wild animal I was. His hand stroked his stubble in thought. "Lucinda? Can you hear me?"

I didn't answer, only continued my struggle.

Six bent down and picked up my foot, cradling the bare flesh in his large mitts. I tried to kick him, but surprisingly enough, he was much stronger than me.

Get your hands off her! I'll kill you! I'll kill you! Jamie was beside himself, having to watch the scene play out with no control over any of it.

Six stroked behind my ankle slowly, but then delivered

a pinch to my tendon that had me thrashing in pain, instead of just for freedom. He released the pressure point and rubbed my foot, speaking quietly so I had to calm down to hear him as I seethed in silence. "Did you feel that? That's painful, right? I don't want to do that, but you leave me no choice when I can't get your attention. I need you to answer me." He stroked the tender spot that made me tense up. "Nod if you understand."

I obeyed, not wanting that all over again.

"Good girl. See? That wasn't so hard. Am I speaking with Lucinda?"

I nodded once.

"Is there a chance you'll let me speak to Hilda? To your mother?" He was on bended knee in supplication, fingers poised over my freezing foot to inflict more pain if I didn't answer.

I mouthed, *I'm not Hilda. I'm not my mom.*

Captain Six smiled that I was answering and calming down enough to communicate. "This must be very confusing for you."

I nodded.

He rubbed my ankle, stretching my foot forward and back to relieve the echoes of the sting. "I wasn't sure when they brought you in, but when I saw you, I knew she'd done it. It's a rare bit of magic, older than laplanding. So few even believed it could be done, but they didn't know Hildy like I did. She took limitations as a challenge. She was amazing like that."

I had no clue what he was talking about, but he seemed to like it when I nodded, so I stuck with that.

He blew warmth onto my toes, and as much as him being near me was upsetting on every level, my freezing skin relaxed involuntarily as he rubbed sensation into my foot. "Are you familiar with the Nøkkendalig?"

I recoiled in disgust, nodding as I clenched my fist.

"If I untie you, will you behave? I don't relish the idea of taking a switch to Hildy's daughter, but I will if you force my hand."

I was horrified at that mental image. I nodded, letting my clenched muscles go limp so there would be no confusion that I would not try to escape.

For now.

Captain Six undid my arm restraints, and the release of blood through my veins was a painful relief. "You needn't worry. The Nøkkendalig don't plague the rivers anymore. You can thank your mother for that. One of her friends, Malin, was taken by them, and the Nøkken did nothing, as is their usual stance on unpleasantness. Look the other way and trust someone will handle it." He gave me a conspiratorial scoff. "Your mother wasn't one who tolerated such complacency, so she set out with a few of us to destroy the Nøkkendalig. My best friend and I were by her side the entire way, along with a handful of soldiers from various regions who were equally sick of their women disappearing into the depths. We slaughtered a great number of the underwater abominations that night." His eyes hardened. "Hildy was the bait, but she was a fighter if I'd ever seen one. They took her and she fought with everything she had. We were all swinging swords and doing everything in our power to end them while keeping her safe. That's how your father and your mother became laplanded." He waved his hand. "But I'm sure you know all that."

I shook my head, my mouth open in surprise. I hadn't thought to ask how Mom and Dad laplanded.

Six raised his eyebrow. "Oh, really? Well, I would have assumed she'd told you everything."

I didn't know about Undraland until last year. She never told me a thing, I mouthed.

Six's eyebrows furrowed. "I'm sure I caught that wrong. Did you mean to say you didn't know about Undraland until last year?"

I nodded, earning an incredulous gasp.

"But then you have no idea who your mother was! Who your parents really were! Do you know who you are?!" He touched his salt and pepper brow, searching for the right place to start. "This... well, no wonder you're fighting so hard against us. You have no idea what's going on."

I nodded, finally allowing a little of my fear to surface in my expression.

Careful, Lucy! He'll say anything to get to his end goal.

I knew that was probably true, but I ignored Jamie, grasping at the serpent in front of me to tell me something

I could hold onto – to give me truth that was pretty to distract from the ugliness of my reality.

"Lucinda, here, let me help you." Before I could acquiesce, Six was lifting me out of the chair and helping me to the bed. I scooted far away from him, as was our understood dance. I didn't want the old man in the bed with me, George Clooney or not. He raised his hands to prove their innocence and sat in the chair at the desk a safe two feet from the foot of the bed.

Six's voice was filled with passion when he spoke. "Your mother was Hilda the Powerful. She understood magic better than most, and had a courageous spirit that could inspire even the most cowardly. When she lost Malin to the Nøkkendalig, that was all it took. She told me she was leaving, and I rallied her followers."

I raised my eyebrow at this.

"Your mother drew quite a few eyes, and those eyes followed her without much coercion. I was one of a long line to get to Hilda's right hand."

I couldn't help but be impressed by Six's account of my mom. Sure, she was awesome, but we moved so often, there was little momentum built in the way of making friends. Thinking of her with followers was a huge leap I couldn't quite picture.

"You think I exaggerate?" he said with a small smile beneath his mustache. "She and I were together more in secret than in public. I treasured every second of our connection. I digress." He leaned forward, resting his elbows on his knees. "I gathered a small group of men and we marched to the river Malin had drowned in. Hilda didn't bat an eye when she choked down the *vatten liv* weed and jumped into the water, but she did scream when they took her down." A shadow of torment crossed his face. "That's a sound you never forget." He sat up straighter. "We all jumped in to attack the Nøkkendalig, slaughtering a fair few in the first go. I was focused on taking their leader down, so I didn't see. I didn't notice anything but the light."

I remembered a bright light just before I was yanked to the surface. I nodded vigorously, pointing to him.

"What? The light? Yes, there was a light. Are you familiar with Kunna Tofs? Will o' the Wisps?"

I shook my head. I couldn't remember Uncle Rick mentioning anything that sounded similar to that in his bedtime stories.

"Kunna Tofs are elves who have gone down into the depths and escaped death at the hands of the Nøkkendalig by using a *bevarande* charm. Only the most powerful can manage it, but when worked effectively, it can make you immortal, though the cost for it is high. A Kunna Tofs escapes death, but they are stuck forever where they enact the *bevarande* charm. Their skin becomes translucent, and while they never die, they never really get to live anymore. It's not a charm that's used often."

Well, that's jacked up. I tried to think of places I wouldn't mind being stuck forever, but even the best Chinese food joint would get boring after a few days.

"Most who die in the Lugn River at the hands of the Nøkkendalig are women, naturally. But there are men who have tried to save them that have died there also. I'd never seen a Kunna Tofs until the day your mother jumped into the river. Understand, the charm is so hard to do, that only those who have the most magic in their blood can execute it. One such elf enacted the *bevarande* charm in the Lugn River. He became what's known as the Will o' the Wisp. He rests on the bottom of the river and traded his ability to float to the surface for his life. So he lives, but in a watery prison far underneath the Nøkkendalig."

I shuddered.

"From what I understand, the Nøkkendalig won't go near him. To touch a Kunna Tofs is dangerous, unless they invite you to touch them. That much magic being traded for continued life has an unstable quality to it."

Six paused his recollection to look into my eyes for something I couldn't give him.

He cleared his throat and continued. "The Nøkkendalig and all of us were afraid of the Kunna Tofs, but your mother wasn't afraid of anything." He smiled in a far-off manner filled with tenderness when he spoke of my mom. I hated him one degree less, which by proxy, made me hate myself one degree more. "She got past the Nøkkendalig and swam to the bottom of the river, awakening the Kunna Tofs and begging him for a portion of his magic, so part of him could live on the surface through her." He chuckled. "I couldn't believe something so simple worked. She promised to use the extra magic to help right some of the wrongs in Undraland, and the Kunna Tofs consented. It took a kiss of the lips, and a blast of light that temporarily blinded all of us, and that was that. When she swam to the surface, the Nøkkendalig swarmed her, attacking with fervor. Now it was personal, since she'd passed by them unscathed."

Six's brown eyes hardened with regret and unrequited vindication. "I was fighting them off and didn't see in time, but my best friend did. He swam to Hilda's aid and plunged his dagger into the heart of the leader of the Nøkkendalig. Of course, he did this at the same time she slit the brute's throat. Rolf didn't mean to lapland with his best friend's girlfriend, but that's what happened. It was not half a year before they fell in love and married. I lost the love of my life and my closest friend in one go."

There was a heaviness that fell over us both, and I knew Jamie could feel the gravity on his end, too. He did his best to reassure me. *You are my syster. That will not happen to us. It would have happened already if it was going to. I love Britta, and you love Jens.*

At the mention of Jens's name, I flinched involuntarily, recalling the shocks that came whenever I'd been treated to a recording of his voice.

Jamie shuddered as well, but fought through it. *You are*

not your mother, and I am not Rolf. We will escape and they'll come find us.

A tear fell onto my cheek, whether from the present doom, the sweet sadness of my mom and dad's union, or the utter impossibility of having normal things like love and marriage when all was said and done.

Captain Six stood and offered me his handkerchief, and the simple gesture of friendship earned him one additional degree of trust that I didn't even bother to hate myself for granting him. I met his eyes to communicate a smidgen of gratitude, and he nodded, sitting on the edge of the bed so he could hold onto my hand. "Your mother was extraordinary."

I offered up a hint of a smile.

He stroked the back of my hand as he resumed his story. "There was a lot the Kunna Tofs gave Hildy. One of those gifts was the ability to capture an echo." He exhaled, retracing his steps to compensate for my utter ineptitude in all things magic. "An echo is a portion of her spirit. It's not her soul, mind you, but her spirit. When you were brought in, I saw the signs immediately. There's no such thing as a Guldy in Undraland, yet here you sit with the blondest hair any Undran's ever seen. You've been jinxed by elf magic, my dear. Your mother put her spirit in you, and your father used his elfish abilities to seal the jinx. It's plain as day to anyone who knew Hildy like I did. She put her echo inside you. So while she's most certainly dead, part of her is alive... in you."

10

THE BARRIER

I began to understand the plight of the common mime when I finally started assembling my bearings. The questions came to me like bubbles in a tub, one after the other, each building on the other before they effervesced and floated into the air between us. I couldn't ask the right question; there were too many to choose from.

Captain Six seemed to understand, so he drove the tell-all forward. "You don't sense her? It would be much like how the Tonttu scum is in your head."

I gave Six a scolding frown to end his Jamie bashing. Then I shook my head to indicate I didn't hear my mom. I mean, I felt her love in me in the same way I kept my dad's, Linus's and Uncle Rick's. They comforted me and made me stronger, but they weren't the voice in my head. That was strictly Jamie.

"Then she's built a barrier to keep you from accessing her echo. I can't imagine why, although, I would guess that would explain why you've shown us no magical aptitude. I'll bet if you ever were taken under by the Nøkkendalig, the Kunna Tofs that gave your mother her magic would recognize you by the imprint of his magic in her. The river would light up to give you the chance to escape. She would lead you to the surface."

Waves and currents of astonishment crashed over me as pieces of the unsolved puzzle shifted into place. I'd wondered what the light was, but I didn't like talking about that day, so I never got my questions answered.

"Of course, that point is moot. We captured the remainder of the Nøkkendalig that night. They were imprisoned straightaway. No doubt you have no idea who they are, which is a blessing, my dear. I'd like to think I left my land devoid of the unforgivable evils as much as I could."

Six took my silence as an invitation to keep speaking, which I guess it was. "Tucker mentioned you didn't have any abilities, though your lineage was vast. Huldra, wind elf, water elf, human and siren? To exhibit nothing is a statistical impossibility. Your mother put a block in you to keep her spirit in place. I'm certain of it." He sat back, his ankle crossing over his knee. "I knew Hildy more than most. She wouldn't risk leaving what was hers unprotected."

My mouth had been open for most of his explanation.

To think of a portion of my mom – more than the ashes Tucker had stolen from me – traveling with me wherever I went was enough to blow my mind in seven uneven pieces.

The captain lifted my hand as if it were made of glass. "Know this: I would recognize my Hildy if she were hidden inside a troll. Part of your treatment has been geared toward breaking the laplanding bond with that Tonttu waste of life, and the other part is to break Hildy free so you can access her abilities and communicate with her. Replace Jamie's voice with hers."

He didn't need a response from me. Six knew I was pretty much toast after that blast. The captain brought my hand to his lips and kissed the back of it like a true gentle-man. Then his hand drifted to my knee, causing me to stiffen. When it climbed up my thigh, I thrashed around to escape the unwelcome ickiness, batting at him and hyper-ventilating through the awful.

Six stilled his hand and squeezed. "Hildy, if you can hear me, I'll do whatever it takes to give you a voice again. I'll keep you with me until you can tell me all the things I've been waiting to hear." Then he kissed the top of my head like a father-figure. "Let me go get you some dinner, darling."

When he left, the door shut behind him, and I knew from the double click that I was locked inside to keep me from escaping. Jamie urged me to use the time to search for weapons or tools we could use to escape, but I was useless.

I could see my near future too clearly. Somehow they would figure out how to break the bond. Jamie would be killed after who knows what kind of torture, and I would be spared. But I would be forced to stay with Captain Six as he tried to coerce my mom to come out and play.

I shuddered at the idea of sharing a body with my mom while she conversed with her ex-lover.

My mom – parts of her, anyway – was alive in my brain. I searched for her, calling out in all the recesses of my mind, but the only thing that came back were imagined images of her. It wasn't real. It was the same level of lucidity I used when daydreaming of Jens, which I didn't do much of anymore.

Jamie and I both flinched at the mention of Jens. I tried to muscle through the knee-jerk reaction of involuntary pain that felt real, but I couldn't get back to that safe place in my mind. There was no bed he spooned me in on the upper level of our perfect home. There was no dancing to cheesy nineties hip-hop – the best kind of hip-hop, by the way – gyrating around the kitchen while we cooked dinner together. I couldn't even picture him with dirt up to his elbows from working in our garden without feeling the jolt of fear from the shocks. I remembered giving him many a glad eye when he came in all dirty and tan with a bowl full of tomatoes and snap peas. What can I say? The man could rock jeans and a t-shirt like it was a 007 tux. You can't not love the man that hoes your garden.

Though I tried to revel in these images and memories,

they hurt me on a physical level, so much that Jamie begged me to stop. He pushed images of Britta at me so I had a friend to distract me from trying to find Jens anymore.

I made her help search for my mom, but it was no use. The block – if it was in fact there as Six insisted – was solid. I couldn't access my powers. I thought back to my blast of roof-demolishing magic that brought my mother's voice to the surface. Now it all started to make sense (in that crazy way *Alice in Wonderland* makes sense). When she'd blown a hole clean through Tucker's roof, it had been to protect me from Tucker bringing my magic to the surface. I hadn't been able to solve that mystery, so I'd shelved it. Now the answer was smacking me in the dumbfounded face.

11

HOW WE WOULD END IT

I'm not sure how long the door remained locked, but Jamie refused food two times, so we guessed at three or four days. Captain Six never returned with the promised dinner, and I couldn't tell if that was a good thing or a very bad thing.

My body was frustrating me. On the one hand, I had the freedom to move around the small room. On the other hand, I hadn't eaten or drank in at least three days, and I was terribly malnourished before that. I resigned myself to lying in the bed. Walking had become too painful on my joints. They felt like unlubricated rusty gears grinding against sharp bone with even the smallest movement.

The door to my room opened, but it wasn't Captain Six. A bald orderly in blue scrubs came around to the bedside and reached for me with greedy hands. I recoiled, shirking to the other side of the bed, my fists flinging out at his face when he bent over the bed and dragged me over to him. Bile and panic rose up in me that I was being taken back to the darkness, back to the cell. I writhed and punched for all I was worth. Perhaps Foss's lessons had taught me to throw a decent punch, but my best effort was no match for Baldy's girth. He acknowledged my resistance as if I was a bothersome fly. I was shoved into the wheelchair, arms and legs strapped in place. I'd gotten in a solid kick, but it only irritated him instead of incapacitating my foe.

A needle was jammed into my arm after the muting collar was slapped back around my neck. I went limp before I could claw it off, praying for my mother to bust out of her shell and rescue me from this never-ending hole.

I AWOKE TO UTTER DARKNESS THAT FILLED ME WITH THE nothingness of a hopeless void with every cold breath I dragged into my aching body. They switched to bottled water in the cells, so Jamie let us drink that. But the food was still tamper-worthy, so we pushed the meals away each time they were sent to us.

Our eternal nothingness was only interrupted by inter-mittent bouts of shock therapy, courtesy of our cell phones that had Jens's voicemails on them. There were cuffs on our calves now that had zapped me so many times, I couldn't feel the muscle move anymore, only a ripping pain I couldn't escape. I had grown to fear the sound of my boyfriend's voice, to wince each time I heard it.

One bowl of refused gruel and only a bottle each of water equaled two days spent chained to the cold concrete floor in my solitary cell.

Three.

Four.

Seven.

At eight, Jamie and I gave up. Half the time we felt deranged from the pain of the shocks that lit our insides up with white-hot agony. I was starting to hallucinate images of Jens flying at me with his knife, running at me with a gun, and punching my deadened calves that had lost all sensation. They shocked us throughout the day, and woke us often in the night, so we could never get a full REM cycle. Sometimes if I even thought of Jens, I felt shocks that weren't even happening. I learned to block him out of my mind completely.

We resumed our deal and stopped drinking the bottled water, so we could speed up our ending. Jamie curled up next to me on the floor of my mind. We were leaning up against the brick wall and the translucent wall that were next to each other toward the back of my brain. Jamie spooned my limp form as we drifted in and out of consciousness. *I'm here, sweetheart. I'm here. Feel the warmth? I'll keep you warm.*

He conjured up my gray squirrel, and David Cassidy burrowed next to my face to keep me company. I shivered in the dark as Jamie muttered incoherently, his mind slipping as mine was.

My arms had been covered by the sadistic sirens to keep me from sight, but they'd ruled my collar unnecessary. My big brother and I were together, and that's how we would end it.

12

THE BEGINNING OF THE END

I flexed my wrists and felt stiffness there. On both arms were those cursed iron cuffs, weighing me down and muting any chance at me tapping into what little magic I might possess deep down inside.

When the bald orderly came for me, I didn't have the strength to resist as he released my fetters, picked me up with great care and strapped me into a wheelchair. The vinyl straps would've been a joke to Foss, but they dug into my thin skin, binding me to their wishes. Every movement caused my brittle bones to grind against each other. I called out for Jamie in my head, but his focus was so intermittent, it was a wasted effort. He moaned inaudibly in response, but offered no advice or comfort. Though we had chosen to die together, we were slowly losing our grip on each other, due to our diminished states.

Fear was constant for me, so this was nothing new. I'd long since run out of tears, so my lower lip quivered soundlessly when a sack was pulled over my head.

"Now, now. It's only to shield your eyes from the lights in the hallway," Baldy told me.

I was wheeled into a dark room I'd not seen before, I realized, as the hood and my gloves came off. I could see enough using my arms as a guide, though I had to squint and close my eyes often to avoid the burn in my retinas. In the center of the room was something I'd only witnessed via Linus's disgusting slasher movies. It was a patient's bed with restraints for the arms and legs.

Like a flipbook, innumerable horrors flashed through my mind, each more gruesome than the last. It was a thing of mercy I'd been eight days without food; I wouldn't last long under whatever torture they had in store for me.

An orderly took me from Baldy, wheeling me next to the bed. His goatee hid his expression and kept his look of scolding tempered at my weak attempts at breaking free. He was strong, with Jamie-sized muscles to lift me – not that he needed them. I was laid onto the bed and strapped down, despite my best efforts to escape. I wasn't sure if I saw correctly, but the orderly's brown eyes hidden beneath matching brown bushy eyebrows and low-hanging hair actually looked guilty at participating in my incarceration. To my temples, he hooked suckers connected to wires that fed into a small machine on a stand behind the bed.

I silently pled for mercy, for help, for anything, but he

left me after placing a rubber guard in my mouth, enclosing me in the room by myself. My hands glittered, giving me just enough light to be able to see that no one was there. I jerked at the restraints, but as with everything thus far, I was ineffectual to save myself.

This is it, Jamie. This is how we die.

Stay strong, he answered back, though it was more of a wish than anything else. Neither of us had even a modicum of strength left. The powers that be had taken off Jamie's iron restraints, but he was too paralyzed to move in his cell. Jamie did the only thing he could to comfort me in my hour of need. He conjured up an image of Linus, who ran to me with urgency befitting my other half. My heart swelled as fake Linus cupped my face, and even though I knew he wasn't real, the security he always gave me was.

We did the best we could, syster, Jamie said.

All I could do was gape at my brother. It was Linus when he was healthy, with a little roundness to his cheeks. The half of me that was missing ached. The agony was almost enough to tear me off the table. Linus stood next to the cold slab I was strapped to and looked at me as if I was wearing an embarrassing hat or something. Linus took his thumb and rubbed it across my forehead. *Well, that's weird. You've got something on your forehead.*

Too many things, I replied. *Don't leave me.*

Linus kissed his thumb and pressed it to the crease between my eyebrows. *You know I never have.*

My forehead burned for a nanosecond, and I saw a flash of my Uncle Rick's serene face looking down on me.

Then it started.

13

LIGHTNING FROM WITHIN AND WITHOUT

*J*amie's voice filled the room, though I knew it was a recording. I had Jamie in my head hearing the same thing, and he was just as baffled as I.

"Lucy, I need you to come over. I can't figure out how to use my remote. The TV's just a blank screen." The message was months old, and I remembered that night well. Teaching Undrans basic human things took a lot of patience and a good sense of humor.

No sooner had I recalled digging into the pumpkin pie Britta had made as Jens walked Jamie through proper use of his TV, did electricity rip through me from the connectors at my temples.

I couldn't scream. The electricity gripped me so hard, I couldn't move. For endless seconds or whole minutes, my back arched unnaturally on the table. I had never known pain of that intensity before. I'd been hurt my fair share of times, but the zero to a million was something no one could have prepared me for.

When the lightning finally released me, I slumped on the slab. I could feel an itch starting in the back of my brain, which was the only distraction from the agony that echoed throughout my veins. This was worse than the bursts of shock we got if we spoke. It was worse than the short eruptions that happened when they played Jens's voice to shock that comfort away from me. Those had not been electrocutions. I knew because I'd been able to wear iron on my wrists, and my arms hadn't singed from the voltage. This was straight up electricity, and I was straight out of my mind from one small blast of it.

Jamie's voice played again. "Hey, *syster*. Britta made us chicken soup. Could you send Jens over to pick up your bowl?"

That recording happened when Jamie and I caught a cold together. Undra's remedies for the common cold were fascinating, but I wasn't up for dipping my feet in scalding water for three minutes, then putting on icy, wet socks underneath heavy wool socks and then going to bed. He'd humored me with chicken soup. I'd humored him with giving myself a pedicure in warm water. He was a good friend.

White spots burst through my vision, and I thought my eyes were going wonky on me. When I opened my eyelids,

I was blinded by a light brighter than my retinas could handle gracefully. Even after shutting my eyes tight, I couldn't escape the sun that seemed to fill the room. My head thrashed left and right, but there was nowhere to hide. I heard Jamie howling in my mind as he cowered on the floor away from the light that plagued us. Linus cupped his hands over my eyes as I flailed about fruitlessly.

Another jolt of electricity, followed by another. With each shock, Jamie was thrown further and further away down the dark hallway that separated our psyches. I wanted to find him and bring him back, but he was lost in the black that kept us apart.

I shouted in my mind for Linus to go after Jamie, but my brother stayed with me. *Do you feel that?* Linus breathed as heat started at my toes. I had a brief reprieve from the pain, but didn't trust the lull. *Can you feel the fire?*

What? What is that? Is it them? Am I on fire? I asked, disoriented and terrified. The room had gone back to black, but my eyes were still aching.

Linus smoothed my dirty hair from my face. *No, weirdo. It's you. Can't you feel it?*

The itchy feeling in the back of my mind near the brick wall and the translucent one grew more insistent, and were my hands not tied down, I would've clawed at my scalp. *What is it? Make it stop! It hurts!*

Linus knew. I don't know how, but he knew what the wall was.

When the hot burst of electricity ripped at my body again, the brick wall shook violently, but the translucent wall exploded in fury, like it had been just waiting for its moment to prove its power. To my surprise, the guy I'd been in the cell with in Elvage stepped out from behind the shambles.

Charles Mace? I asked, confused as to why my mind conjured him up in my last moments. His lanky form made its way to my bedside, standing next to Linus and placing his hand over mine. His silver irises looked deep into my eyes, as if willing me to remember things I didn't have access to.

And then it hit me like a wave from a hurricane that sucked me into its vortex. I was small, and the water kept crashing over my head, dragging me under until I was drowning in information that had no place to rest in my brain. The facts jumped around like popcorn in my mind, making me motion sick and terrified beyond what I could handle.

Charles Mace was my brother from when my parents lived in Undraland before I was born.

They left him in Alrik's care when the Huldras were banished.

He'd been fitted with a collar to keep him from whistling. It was a lot like the collar I was wearing now.

I'd lifted Kristoffer's key that took Mace's collar off.

I'd held his hand and held him as he tried to declare himself and grow from lurky loner into a man who could run with Jens the Brave, a prince and a Fossegrimen chief.

He'd been the one who opened the farlig fisk's mouth.

He'd been the one who'd kept me from drowning in the boat's hull.

Charles Mace had been the one...

He'd been my brother. Flashes of memories filed themselves in order quicker than I could make sense of them. Then suddenly my mind stopped at the prison in Elvage. Huddled on the ground, holding hands like children as our last moments ticked by. I vowed I wouldn't leave him. I wouldn't be the family that abandoned him.

And yet, I had. My lips parted as I looked up into the face of the man who'd truly loved me enough to give himself up for me. Only one word birthed from my cracked and dry lips. *Why?* I mouthed, mourning his loss with grief over the situation I just barely understood.

Because I love you. Mace spoke to me as if the answer should have been obvious, but love like that was too grand for one person to keep. I would never be able to earn or deserve his sacrifice, and yet he'd given it to me without asking anything in return.

You were always a beautiful thing, he commented, looking at my besotted state as if I was the sun and moon. It absolutely smashed my already obliterated heart, and I reached a new level of my silent version of wailing. He bore a look of bold determination as he stood next to Linus. *I won't see you broken like this. Here's where we fight.*

I sobbed openly in my imagination. *We? I can't move! And you're not real! You... you died, Mace! I just stood there and let them take you away! I'm so sorry! How that must've hurt you to hear me say I didn't know you. You died hearing that! Forgive me! I can't stand it!* I thrashed around on the table again, my heart bursting and breaking. Even the electricity coursing through me wasn't enough to wipe the anguish from me. I'd lost two brothers.

Mace scolded me as if I was playing a game and being obstinate on the rules. *Your feet. You feel that, right?*

Yeah. It's hot. What is it?

It's the power inside you that you haven't been able to access. Water elf, wind elf, siren, Huldra and human. It's all swirling inside you. You're just missing one thing. Linus switched places with Mace, and Charles began running his fingers through my hair, pressing on my forehead to ease the itch that had been bothering me. *Do you feel that scratch? Do you see that brick wall?*

Well, yeah. It's been in the back of my mind for a while now, but I don't remember ever putting it there.

Mace kissed my forehead. *Tear it down, sweet girl. Tear it to the ground. Behind there lies more power than anything anyone could do for you.*

I thought about the logistics of tearing down a brick wall and conjured up a sledgehammer that was light enough to lift with some level of competence. *Linus? I can't move.* For all my imagination acrobats, I couldn't envision past my restraints. Blame it on the constant electrocution.

On it! Linus assured me, picking up the tool and aiming it like a superhero's fated weapon. Three swings, and he made a dent.

Four, and he made a hole.

Turns out, a hole was all I needed.

14

HILDA THE POWERFUL

Heat ran up my limbs and filled my body. Suddenly, I wasn't Lucy Kincaid. I was Lucy the Destroyer. My body was still a wasted shell, but something primal awakened in me I didn't realized I possessed.

It was Undraland.

It was my mother.

The wall she'd put up in my mind to keep my genetic abilities at bay had just enough of a gap in it to allow a rush of her to flood through me, and for me to catch a glimpse of the determination on her face. In my mind, I could smell her subtle flowery perfume that ripped my heart out when my brain registered the change.

A whistle I had never been able to tap into burst out of me like a punch to the stale air of the torture chamber I was being held in. I couldn't control it. I didn't even know I was doing it. It was my mom.

With dark curly hair and too much moxie to be held down by death, my mom shouted through the hole in the brick wall of my mind. *Open your eyes, darling! I can get us out, but I have to see where we're going.*

My eyes opened to the room that was lit only by my hands. I blinked a few times, pushing through the pain so I could grasp the overwhelming crush and crash of seeing my mother and Mace again.

The goateed orderly burst into the room, along with a handful of doctors and people in uniforms. The whistle coming out of me took the wind from their sails, and one by one, they collapsed on the ground. My mother controlled the whistle that flowed from me; I simply owned the lips. She revived only Goatee, and coerced him into undoing my ties.

But I can't move! I'm barely alive, Mom! I sobbed to her.

Hold on, baby! she cried.

It was my mother. Her voice. The pride in her tone when she called me "baby". It was her all over.

I ran to her. I thought of nothing else but her as I fell to my knees in front of the hole, with Linus and Mace at my sides. There wasn't more than a large fist-shaped hole through the wall, but it was enough to make me near hysterical to get to her. *Mom! Mama! We can get you out!*

No, you can't, and don't try to do any more with the sledge-hammer. This is a one-time deal, baby, so let's make it a good one.

I reached through the hole and snatched at her hand,

holding the fingers that were so similar to mine tighter than what could be comfortable.

Goatee lifted my body off the table, carried me out into the hall and placed me in my wheelchair. He turned off the lights in the concrete hallways, so I could see using the light of my hands, which was at the maximum of what I could handle.

Jamie! Mom, I don't know where Jamie is, but we have to find him! Jamie and I are laplanded, so I can't leave without him.

I'll take care of it, she assured me as she'd done when I was accused of cheating on a Chemistry exam in the tenth grade. I'd been on the brink of suspension, and the next day, I was being apologized to by the teacher and principal.

Whatever, I'd earned that A. Ask the farlig fisk. I rock at science.

Yes, you did, honey. Now try to keep your eyes open so I know where to tell the orderly to steer us.

I kept my eyes open, but retreated into my head where my mom, Linus and Charles were. Charles scooped me in his wiry arms like I weighed nothing, and brought me tight to his side. I dreamt up a soft cushiony blanket that he wrapped me in, and just like that, I was safe again. I was good at imagining warmth, and the blanket was a sentimental tool that helped me muscle past the freeze my extremities shuddered at.

My whistle changed, and Goatee wheeled me down another corridor not two hundred feet from where I'd been strapped to the bed. He unlocked the door and opened it, revealing my poor Jamie, a broken pile of dirty, hairy limbs on the concrete floor. Goatee left for a few minutes, returning with another orderly who had a shaved head and a second wheelchair.

Jamie was dragged by the men and hefted into the chair. He was drooling into his overgrown beard, and had no idea I was next to him. I seemed to be experiencing a separation between my body and my brain, but Jamie was in his own world entirely. I wanted to hold him, but I could only picture the state my own body had been reduced to.

My mom's whistle shifted, and the men wheeled us down several hallways, leading us steadily upward and to the left. Every now and then, the floors inclined at a slight angle I hadn't noticed before, and I knew my mom had done it.

All sirens, my mom gasped as we passed a lunch room of sorts. They fell like autumn leaves at her whistle, a scattered mess of an underground kingdom. They had been more powerful than Undraland could handle, but to humanity, they were mole people. They all fell at the feet of my mother. Perhaps if they'd had an inkling that a practicing Huldra was amongst them, they could've taken precaution and put my collar back on me. But now it was too late. Hilda the Powerful had the upper hand.

She had me.

Goatee abandoned my chair when we reached what looked like the communal restrooms – you know, for those lucky jaggoffs who weren't forced to pee into a bucket. He ran in and turned on all the faucets and showers on full blast before coming back to me.

My mom drew on latent powers in me I'd never been able to hone. Suddenly, I was Lucy the Water Elf, and hot liquid poured out of my bony hands. Buckets and buckets of angry water streamed behind me as Goatee and Baldy pushed our chairs up the slow incline toward the surface of wherever we were. I could scarcely operate my hands, but my mom knew what to do.

She always knew what to do.

When I'd almost been suspended for allegedly cheating on that exam, she'd known what to do. When I'd skinned my knee or gotten a cold, she'd known what to do. Today was no different.

The wall she'd constructed to keep her powers away from me left her in control of the abilities I'd acquired. She'd been collecting them, studying them, and knew exactly how she would use them to set me free. I'm not sure why I didn't expect as much. I mean, come on. She's a Kincaid girl.

More water than I could fathom shot out of me, bursting from my hands and now my feet. Baldy and Goatee slipped a few times, but mom kept their feet determined.

A gasp of hesitance came from my mother. *Six? Lucy, is Sixten of the Greenhaven living here?*

A shudder ripped through me on the inside. *Yes. He's*

Captain Six now. Boy does he have the burning loins for you. He's the one who knew you were inside me.

My mom swallowed, closed her eyes and nodded. Part of her heart swooned – I could feel her swing of emotion – and I cringed. Mom and Dad were the only ones that made sense together. I didn't like this Six character making my mom feel so teenager-ish.

Mom's voice was clear through the hole in her brick wall. *I cannot let him die.* Her whistle changed, and our orderlies stopped. Baldy ran back the way we'd come, shouting out for Captain Six as he went. He returned two whole minutes later, during which my heart pounded that we would be apprehended. Goatee surrendered me to Six, who ran my wheelchair forward with Baldy pushing Jamie's. Goatee made himself useful opening doors and turning off lights.

Be careful, Mom. Six hates Jamie. Don't let him hurt Jamie. In a careful tone, I said, *Are you sure Six should be saved? He let them keep me here!*

My mom's reply was desperate. *I can't just let him die! I couldn't save him the first time during the slaughter. I thought he* had *died! Now that I have a second chance? I must save him. He was your father's closest friend.*

I knew better than to argue further, but I had so much more to say on the subject. I wanted to give my mom a twenty-minute rant on the creepiness Six had devolved to. I wanted to shake sense into her.

In my brain.

It was hard to keep up with what was actually going on.

Goatee wheeled me to, of all things, a crude lift rigged on a system of ropes and pulleys. Despite their detailed torture devices, the sadistic Sirens had yet to install a proper elevator. Goatee wheeled us onto the square wood platform, and Six grabbed the ropes.

My body paused whistling to take a breath, and I registered that someone was running up behind us toward the lift's platform. My wheelchair turned around, revealing two men in scrubs with their hands over their ears as they charged us.

I have seen my mother enraged on precious few occasions. One was when she heard our high school teacher was referring to her son as "Chemo Kid". Another was when Linus discovered the front desk hadn't turned off the free porn channel at one of the skeezier motels we stayed at. If I respected her then, I feared her now. She was not one to be trifled with, and someone was screwing with her whistle's effect.

She couldn't control them, but she could sure as anything order the man who'd carried a torch for her all these years. Six ran at the men, swinging his well-trained fists that yearned to be put to proper use.

Goatee continued pulling us upward until I could only see the shoes of one of the men as he was flung over Six's shoulder like it was nothing. We reached a new corridor that had a lower ceiling not built for the comfort of

Undrans. Goatee and Baldy had to duck as they ran us onward.

Mom seethed through her hole in the brick wall of my mind. *Lucy, summon your father here right this instant! And your uncle, too.*

15

ROLF OF THE GREENHAVEN

I did as she ordered without question, casting up a "yikes" look at Mace. He wasn't looking at me, though. His stare was fixed at the hole where he could see more of his mother than he had since he'd been a baby. Though he held me, he yearned for her. His gaze was only distracted by the sight that made my heart leap.

My dad. Rolf Kincaid in the imaginary flesh burst into my brain like a superhero, chest barreled and hands at the ready. His hair was done up like Clark Kent's, as he used to wear it when he took my mom out for the rare date night. *Lucy? Honey? I'm here! I'm here!*

Though I could conjure up his image anytime I wished, I tried not to think of my parents. It was too painful to see their faces and know I'd never have them with me again. I hadn't allowed myself to think of my dad in months – at least, not more than replaying a memory.

Conversations with the dead were reserved for Linus. He already knew I was nine kinds of crazy.

My dad ran to Charles and me, catching us both up in a hug that felt like breathing and smelled like the home I never left home without. Dad clutched my frail form in a hug that squeezed the emotion out of me in a gut-twisting scream that echoed across the corners of my mind. It was too many feelings to compartmentalize. My dad with his smile that was only given to kindness, my mom, here but still held back by her own powers, Linus with his... everything I needed, and Mace, poor Mace, with all the memories he'd made me forget stuffing themselves back inside my brain like too many tickets in a raffle box.

Uncle Rick came to the party soon after and touched my forehead lovingly with his thumb. *Up you get,* he said, and just like that, my imagination worked overtime. I was able to stand with new strength, but my movements were jerky, like a badly edited horror movie where the drunken sorority girl is stumbling through a strobe-lit party with the killer in tow. In fact, my whole brain began to flicker, as if the lights were being turned on and off in my consciousness. I friggin' hate strobe lights.

My dad ran to my mom, and the sight did my heart good. He was hers to tap into now. I did my job, which was getting him to our little pretend family reunion. They were holding hands through the hole and shouting to each other, but I couldn't make out the words. My dad's free arm went around Mace, gripping him as if Charles was his only link to breathing properly. He even let out an angst-filled bleat of agony into Mace's dark hair. Linus clamped a hand down on my dad's shoulder, and my heart was filled to bursting. It was my family as we were meant to be.

The water shooting out from my body was so loud now; it was hard to hear much else. After the lift, the orderlies were steering Jamie and I down the low-ceilinged corridor toward a dead end. I began to panic, but when we reached it, I looked up and saw a manhole cover. Goatee boosted Baldy up, who popped open the lid to the outside.

The strobe light in my brain was maddening. I could tell it was blinking in conjunction with my level of available brainpower left, and that my body was on its last leg of survival. I'd been starved, electrocuted over and over, kept in darkness and isolated from humanity. I was kind of proud of myself for holding out as long as I had. I knew if I passed out now, the whistle that was getting us out would fade. The orderlies would stop obeying my mother's commands, the sirens would take us back under for more torture, and we would die. I wouldn't get back this clarity again that allowed my entire family to exist together in one room. No matter the plane of reality, the sight of all of us working together was precious to me.

Hurry, Mom! I shouted through the haze of off-and-on lights. *I can't hold on much longer!*

Just a few more minutes, honey! I can get you out! I can help! Linus, hold my hand! Rolf, grab both our boys' hands!

Alrik, hold Mace's hand! Form a chain, everyone! Lucy, hold onto your uncle!

I reached for Uncle Rick, who gripped my palm with a steady expression. From my mother to me, our entire family stood as a unit. Heat began to fill me from the spot where I was holding onto Uncle Rick and flooded into my stomach, and I knew it was a mixture of magic and my emotions swelling beyond the breaking point. The lights began flickering, and I felt myself starting to fade.

Then I heard him.

Linus, figment of my imagination though he was, always knew what to do. He started singing *Safety Dance* in time with the lights, reviving me just enough for a coughed-out laugh. My dad groaned, as he had when Linus and I sang the tune ad nauseum one of the times Linus was confined to the hospital and we missed our high school's dance. Linus grinned through the strain of the magic flowing through him. *Come on, Dad! You can dance if you want to!*

Knock it off, Linus! Mom shouted. *I'm trying to concentrate! Lucy, don't let yourself pass out, honey. Hold on!*

I gritted my teeth and closed my eyes against the flickering light that predicted my impending doom. Alrik squeezed my hand, and I felt his power flowing through me like warm carbonation popping through my veins.

Baldy climbed out of the hatch, letting a flood of fresh nighttime air into the tunnel that temporarily revived me. An alarm had been triggered, but the finish line was in sight. Goatee lifted me up to Baldy, who laid me down on the green grass next to Jamie. My prince was still unconscious with drool crusted in his beard. Goatee handed the collapsed wheelchairs up to Baldy, and then hefted himself out of the hole. Then the two blue-scrub men set about putting Jamie and I back in our easiest mode of transportation.

My mom thought of everything. Every Easter she would hard boil eggs and have us dye them together to eat in our lunches for the next week. Not many teenagers still dyed eggs, but we were always supercool like that. It was the details that made her awesome. Remembering to put a mint in our lunches the days she packed us tuna sandwiches. Writing little love notes inside the napkins. Today it was the details that kept us going. She whistled the orderlies to run us toward the gas station I saw in the distance. Though it was the dead of night, the neon signs were blinding. My eyes gave my mom only just enough information to go on before they shut involuntarily.

My parents were arguing, which they didn't do a whole lot of in front of us.

You know I'm right, Hildy! He has to be destroyed. He kept our daughter and let them torture her just as much as the rest of them.

I can't do it! My mom sobbed. *After all he's been through? How can you ask me to do such a thing?*

My dad's hand reached through the hole and gripped hers tight. *He's a threat to Lucy. Look at what they did to her!*

Six loved you, but not enough to love what was precious to you. He hurt your only daughter. You have to see that!

My mom paused, and then the whistle changed. *You're right, Rolf. I'll take care of it.* It was a mournful tune that told Goatee to head back to the hole.

Baldy parked our chairs near a minivan that was filling up at the pump. All it took was a few seconds of whistling for the woman to happily invite us into her van and hand us her cell phone.

There was an explosion behind us, and then fire and sparks shot up from the manhole. I cringed against the light, closing my eyes again as Jamie was buckled in.

I was laid on the floor of the minivan, and our chairs were stowed in the trunk. Baldy made a phone call on her cell while the woman drove us toward the freeway. I heard screams in the distance and searched inward for an explanation.

Water conducts electricity, my mother explained, her voice choked up. *That's why I had you flood their coven. They'll be dead for real this time.*

My dad held my mom's hand to comfort her. *I know, Hildy. I know.*

I didn't do it to exterminate a whole race! I didn't want that! I did it because they kidnapped my daughter! she cried.

My dad comforted my mom, and it was a beautiful thing to watch. I'd missed the sight of his quiet strength, and her drawing serenity from it.

I peeked at my surroundings in the minivan. Jamie was

slumped in the backseat, completely limp. I was on the floor in front of the middle bench, since my mom was afraid of me being seen in case any sirens had escaped. Baldy was in the front passenger's seat, unbuckled as we drove along at a high speed.

The strobe lights flickered more slowly, and I knew that with my ebbing adrenaline, I would be passing out soon.

Lucy, I need you to listen to me. Listen close, honey. I need you to do something for me. It's Linus. When I crossed over to Undraland, I begged the Mouthpiece to save Linus, to get Pesta to exchange your father and I for him.

I know, I said with bitterness in my tone. *And then she took you into Be and Linus died in my arms. Great plan.*

I felt my mom's wince. *Pesta didn't renege. She gave me some of her magic that binds souls. Before Linus died, I used a bit of it on him. I knew he wouldn't last much longer, so I bound his soul in a vial and got it to your uncle by way of the crematorium. All he knows is that they gave you Linus's ashes, but it's not ashes, honey. It's Linus's soul.*

I had to be hearing things. I couldn't begin to force her words to make sense.

She hurried on, knowing she had mere moments before our time was over. *My spirit's inside of you, keeping your powers at bay, but Linus's soul is in the ashes you were given. Please tell me you have the ashes!*

Tucker! I cried, frantic. *Tucker took my necklace that has the ashes of all my family in it. Linus is in there?*

Yes! Good girl, Lucy! That's wonderful! Linus was never cremated. I only whistled Alrik into thinking he was. I whistled your uncle to steal Linus's body just after he passed and take it to Undra. He buried it, darling. You need the body and the soul! Find Tucker and get Linus's soul back. Then take the soul to the body so they can reunite.

What? How?! You have to know how crazy you sound!

My mom paid my disbelief no mind. She was under the wire. *I had Alrik bury Linus in Nøkken, fifty paces west of the Salmon Seesaw. Tell me you understand! Take the soul to the body, pour it into his mouth, get an elf to do a bonding charm, and he'll come back to you.* When I didn't answer through the slow-motion strobe effect, she yelled, *Repeat it back to me! I won't last much longer, Lucy! Once you pass out, the wall will rebuild and my spirit will keep your abilities away from you.*

Why, Mom? Why can't I have the magic you do?

My mom's voice took on the tone of the last warning before she pulled over the car to give us what-for when we were misbehaving on road trips. *Repeat the instructions, Lucy!*

Fine! I get the ashes from Tucker, dig up Linus fifty paces west of the Salmon Seesaw in Nøkken. I pour the soul ashes into his mouth, have an elf do a bonding charm, and he'll come back to life. Now tell me why you won't let me be like you!

The lights went on in my mind once more, and my mother sighed, holding onto my dad's hand. She blew out a whistle through me in lieu of answering my many desperate questions.

I opened my eyes. The next thing I saw was Baldy in the front passenger's seat, opening the door and leaping out onto the freeway.

Then the strobe light faded to black.

16

JENS, BUT NOT JENS

I hadn't possessed the ability to quantify time in... well, not for quite a while. My mom had managed to push out one last burst of a whistle from me to communicate to the civilian we'd kidnapped to stay with us, just before I passed the smack out.

I hadn't dreamt, but in my unconsciousness, I did finally find Jamie. He was curled in a ball like a cat on the floor of my darkened dream. The dark was terrifying, but it was all we knew anymore. Even the smallest bit of light was painful. I walked over to Jamie in the shared hallway of my mind and curled up next to him. He shifted, and I scooted into his arms so my back was pressed to his stomach. His breath in my stringy hair was shallow and ragged, but it was there, and I'd never smelled anything sweeter. He was thinned and limp, but he was alive. We were alive.

No one else was in my subconscious. The wall had

been repaired and my mother tucked behind it, like she wasn't even there. Uncle Rick, my dad, Mace and Linus were all gone, though my mother's instructions rang clear in my head.

When I finally awoke, it was to the sound of the radio playing lovey nineties soft rock. We were parked outside a convenience store, and it was still dark out. My eyes hurt from the fluorescence coming off the obnoxiously green sign, so I shut them immediately. My body had been in such a constant state of agony that I barely registered the aches anymore. When I lifted my head, I heard an unsettling crack that warned me not to move anything at all. I was on the floor of the minivan, and Jamie was still slumped in the backseat. My thin scrubs offered no warmth in the night, but the heater was on, and the difference it made was heavenly.

The red-haired woman was seated at the wheel, popping her gum and awaiting further instructions. My slight movement drew her eye, and she smiled, turning fully around in her seat to look at me. "You're awake? Finally. Sorry, I turned on the music because I got bored. Did I wake you?"

I pointed to my throat, indicating I couldn't talk.

Her shoulders slumped. "Your friend should be here by now. Jenny? The voice told me to take you here and wait until Jen came and got you. The man who jumped out the door on the freeway said your friend would be picking you up here at four, and it's four-twenty." She double-popped the piece of gum in her mouth. "Who was he? Weird that he jumped out of the van and died."

I shook my head and closed my eyes again to fend off the light.

"Your arms have glitter paint on them. Did you want to go inside and wash up? They have a bathroom, I'm sure."

I shook my head again. I hadn't been part of a real conversation in a while.

"I'm starved, but I have to stay with you until Jenny comes." She scrunched her wide nose as she informed me of the inconvenience. Being that I had actually been starved, I didn't have a ton of sympathy at the moment.

Before she could ask another question I didn't have an answer to, I heard the scariest sound that ever was. A car peeled into the parking lot, a door slammed and Jens called my name. My heart stuttered and spluttered, but I couldn't pick myself up to get away from him. I lifted my hand and pointed to the voice, motioning for the woman to get me away from the shock that would surely accompany the illusion that was Jens.

"Finally!" She honked the horn and flagged Jens down.

Jens flung open the door, revealing messy black hair and muscles bulging more than a man had a right to. The terror filled my limited vision before I had to shut my eyes against the added light from the neon of the few businesses across the street.

The shocks. Oh, the shocks. I knew they were sure to come, and my body jerked at the phantom voltage. The hallucinations of me suffering at his hands. I grimaced and shirked away from him.

"Lucy! What did they do to you? How did..." The sweetest voice in all the world sounded scared and horrified.

I wanted to go to him, but knew the pain would come if he was near me. That was always the way of it. Hear his voice, then writhe in pain.

Jens's voice now was dripping with emotion. "Foss, grab Jamie! Hurry! Let's get a move on now! We've got no idea who's behind them or how much of a lead we've got." Jens climbed in, but looked almost afraid to touch me. His hands shook as they ghosted over my body, guessing at how to lift me without shattering what was left of me. "Baby, baby," he whispered, shaking his head. "I'm sorry. I'm so sorry. I've got to move you, but I'll be so gentle. Just a little jostle. Hang on."

I saw a tear fall from Jens's unshaven cheek down onto my shirt, and guessed he might actually be really there – in real life, not in my head. That the rescue was, in fact, happening. With all the people who'd been running around in my imagination, it was hard to tell for sure. When Jens lifted me off the floor, everything throbbed anew. I bit my crusted and dry lip against the jarring agony, knowing I'd been stupid to trust that the memory of Jens wouldn't sting. My bones felt like they were grinding against each other as he moved me. Every bit of me hurt, and it was thinking about Jens that did it. Oh, how I wished it wasn't true, that he was real and the agony didn't flood me whenever I heard his voice. Jens in real life didn't hurt me, but this one did, so I knew it couldn't be him. *Right?*

When he edged me out of the van, my eyes shut and I turned my face into his chest. He smelled like sugar cookies. It had to be Jens. I'd been wishing with everything in me that he'd come for me. It felt too good to be true.

It felt like a trap.

I struggled against him, terrified to be near the source of what was sure to be more torment. "I'm sorry!" Jens moaned. "Am I hurting you? Tell me how to help you! Tell me what hurts, what's broken, so I don't break it more."

Was I in the minivan, or was I still chained to the concrete floor? When was the jolt coming? I wished they would just get to it; the anticipation was killing me.

I poked around in my head for signs of my family, but they'd all disappeared. Surely if my mom was still here, she could tell me if Jens was real or not.

My mom? Why did a wall with my mom behind it feel more real than anything else? It sounded crazy. Maybe I was crazy. Dig up a body I'd already had cremated? How could that be real?

Jens carried me to our car and sat in the backseat with my limp body lolling in his lap. I vaguely recalled how it felt to lie in my boyfriend's lap. We'd watched movies together in this very position in our living room every Tuesday night. I hadn't been so feeble then. There was no romance or sensuality to this. Jens sobbed openly over me, rocking back and forth gently to soothe either me or himself, I wasn't sure. It felt like Jens. It looked like Jens. I hadn't been shocked yet.

Yet.

Was I still locked in the cell?

I heard Britta's voice shrieking, but everything was so distorted. Normal sounds boomed at odd pitches and volumes. Jamie was slid in next to us, and I heard Britta wailing, "Jamie, Jamie, Jamie, Jamie!" over and over.

Foss's voice reached my ears, and my chin leaned toward the sound. I hadn't let myself think of Foss in so long; his gruff cadence sounded so real. "The driver's been controlled by a Huldra. She doesn't know anything other than what the guy on the phone told us."

"Fine." Jens spoke through his tears. "Foss, go grab them some bottles of water and whatever passes for food in there. Quick, and then we're out." The door shut and Jens gently pressed his fingers to different spots on my limbs, testing them to assess their levels of disuse. It was terribly painful, so I guessed this was how the sirens were torturing me this time. "Baby, can you hear me? Open your eyes, Loos. I need to know you're awake and alive."

I obeyed, but we were parked under a streetlight that was too bright, so he only got a peek at my eyes. I wondered if the food they'd given us caused hallucinations. The neon color danced with snippets of the face I loved that caused phantom jolts of electricity to shoot through me.

Phantom or real? I couldn't tell the difference anymore.

Suddenly I was being sat up and water was lightly trickled into my mouth. I swallowed reflexively, pained at the motion that should have been simple. I felt the car jostle as it started down the road.

"Loos, don't go to sleep, baby. You have to eat." Jens's voice was so tearful, that I obeyed. He pried open my mouth and placed two fingers onto my tongue. Creamy peanut butter stuck to the roof and sides of my mouth. More water, then more peanut butter. The taste was like nothing I could have dreamed, though I'd yearned a great many times for food of this quality in the cell. Did that mean I was out of the cell? Peanut butter stuck to my tongue. It certainly wasn't the tapioca oatmeal slop. It wasn't poisoned. It wouldn't cut me off from Jamie.

Would it?

My eyes flew open and I searched for Jamie. He was sucking on Britta's peanut buttered fingers with his eyes closed, not even aware of what he was doing.

When Jens tried to feed me the fifth bite, I shirked away, wary of what poison lurked in the delicious spread.

"What? Did you want something else? More water? Foss got you trail mix, crackers, and about half the store. Tell me what happened, Loos!" Jens was distraught, desperate for answers. "At least tell me who had you!"

I was unsure. It looked like Jens. Well, it was a worn

ragged version of the superhero I adored, at least. He was wild, unshowered and had a half-inch beard masking part of his face.

When he tried to feed me again, my breath began to quicken. I couldn't escape them. They would feed me until the poison made me forget Jamie. If I couldn't find Jamie, I'd never last long enough for anyone to find me.

No one was coming for me.

But... but...

"Baby, it's okay! Calm down. I've got you!"

I tried to fend off the hands that forced more water into me, but they were so much stronger. I would forget Jamie again, and they'd keep me in the dark forever. I wouldn't go out like that without a fight.

"I'm sorry! I looked everywhere, but I *still* don't know where they were holding you. Was it a 'they'? Who had you? I haven't stopped in months! We followed your star, but it hasn't moved, and you weren't anywhere! Was Tucker with you? We can't find him, either! What happened, Loos?!"

I watched him as if through a fog. He was beyond any level of stress I'd ever seen him at. He had bags under his crazed emerald eyes and his beard was scraggly. He leaned down to kiss my forehead, but when his whiskers brushed my skin, it reminded me of Captain Six. I cringed and struggled to get away, panicked he would try to make me his wife because of my mom's spirit inside of me.

Now that sounded crazy for sure. Maybe I was just

locked in the cell still. Maybe there was no minivan or mom spirit. Maybe I was just delusional from starvation and dehydration. That made more sense than anything.

"What's wrong? Did you not want me to kiss you?" When Jens took in my confusion and fear, his mouth fell open in horror. "You... Do you know who I am?"

I met his thunderstruck gaze hesitantly as I tried to decipher how to answer that. It looked like Jens. It smelled like Jens. But it fed me, and I couldn't feel Jamie in my head. There was a trap.

They were going to shock me again. At any second, the electricity would light my insides on fire. I tensed against the blast, closing my eyes to brace myself for the jolt.

But it didn't come.

Jens looked sick and sad. Tears fell down his cheeks again, each one a declaration of a broken heart. "That's okay. We can work with that. It's alright." He held onto me possessively. "*I* know who *you* are, and that's all that matters."

17

IT WAS JENS

 don't remember falling asleep, but when I awoke, we weren't in the car anymore. I was in a dark room again.

I knew it. I knew it hadn't been real Jens. Don't eat the food.

The concrete felt soft beneath me. I felt around and put several facts in order with clarity I hadn't had in a long time. I was in a bed that wasn't a cot. The air didn't smell stale, like the underground lair of doom. I was wearing gloves that covered my arms.

Something was attached to my upper arm. I looked up and saw an IV. The bag hanging read Saline, so my fears that I was being pumped full of poison died down a modest amount.

I reached for Jamie in my mind, running to the corners and down our joint hallway calling his name. *Jamie! Jamie?* When he didn't answer, I tried not to panic. Perhaps he was sleeping. If I stopped eating, he would come back to me. We had a system.

The darkness was a thing I was used to, but the room before me when I opened my eyes again wasn't pitch black. There was a sliver of light from the hallway trickling in from under the door, lighting just enough for me to be able to read the bold block letters on the IV bag, but not too bright I couldn't bear it. I shifted on the bed and tried to sit up. I wasn't as weak as I had been, but I still couldn't go anywhere on my own. I knew somehow I had to get out. If I was alone, who knew how long I'd be here before they'd send someone in to drug me.

Someone made a patting noise to my left. I turned and saw Jamie in a bed next to mine. My heart soared when I saw his eyes open and him trying to get my attention by banging his hand on his bed.

Jamie! Jamie! I sobbed in my mind, relieved to see the face I'd only been able to imagine for months.

He reached out to me, but our beds were about three feet apart. I extended my arm and brushed my quaking fingers to his. The contact made both of us tear up. We needed more, so we inched toward the edges of our beds. I dropped my legs over the side and tried to stand. I knew it was a bad idea seconds before I fell, but the smack to the carpet was still jarring.

Carpet?

One of the suckers I didn't even realize was attached to my chest ripped off like a glued-on sticker, and the IV tore out of my arm, but I was that much closer to Jamie, so it didn't matter.

Jamie, sweet Jamie, did the same, tumbling next to me in a pile of ungraceful limbs. We breathed heavily, sinking into each other's arms with teary-eyed relief. Just like that, I found him in my mind again. *Jamie, where are we?*

I thought you knew! I only just woke up. Why are we in the same room? What are they going to do to us next? Don't eat the food, Lucy! Don't eat a thing!

I won't. I'm sorry I caved. We clung to each other in reality and in our brains.

The door opened and a heavy-set brunette woman in pink scrubs came in, fretting when she saw us on the floor. She ran back out and called down the hall for help. *Don't let them take me!* I screamed, gripping Jamie with everything in me. *Jamie, help!*

I won't leave you! Stay strong!

The woman came running back in with…

It was Jens. I think. He turned on the light, causing Jamie and I to do our impersonations of the Wicked Witch of the West melting in toil and desperation.

"No? What's wrong? Is the light too bright?" Jens asked.

I nodded, but was instantly unsure if I should interact with the man who I was too lost to have hope was Jens. The lights went off to our great relief, and Jamie and I clung to each other greedily, bracing ourselves for the moment we would be torn apart and thrown back into the oppressive nothingness. The nurse touched my arm, and I recoiled from the contact, slapping and lashing out as best I could. Jamie was all I had left, and I wouldn't go down without a fight.

"I have to fix her IV," the woman explained, exasperated when I threw a four-limbed fit after she tried touching me again.

"Okay. Let me try." Jens bent down, kneeling half a foot from my feet. It was a distance safe enough to where I didn't feel like he was going to snatch me away from Jamie, but close enough that I could see the details of his face. "Lucy, it's Jens. Do you know who I am?"

I burrowed my back into Jamie's possessive embrace, looking sideways at Jens.

It had to be Jens. It said it was Jens. Why would it lie? Jamie was scared, but he was also desperate. He wanted the mirage to be real, for us to have been rescued.

I regarded the bearded man before me warily, reluctant to declare him friend or foe. I watched his handsome face, the earnest eyes that were etched with hurt and the hands that were raised in surrender.

It was Jamie who made the decision for us. *I have to try. Brace yourself, in case I'm wrong and it shocks us. I think it's Jens.*

No, Jamie! It's not Jens!

Syster, I have to try. He reached around me, extending a shaking hand to his best friend. When Jens reached out to take it, I winced at the small advance, my calves instantly on fire with the phantom shocks I'd been subjected to. I could see the painful effect this had on Jens when his expression dimmed as if I'd cussed him out. I didn't want to hurt Jens.

I was firm. *But it's not Jens. It has a beard.*

Jamie squeezed his best friend's hand, his chest heaving with relief and grief. We'd lost so much time and too much of ourselves. The hope that this was real was a hard truth to accept, but Jamie was stronger than me. When he tried to sit up, Jens moved quickly over to assist him. He was gentle, taking the smallest movement into consideration, knowing we had limited mobility. It was a kindness the real Jens would have known to do. Jens loved Jamie.

And just like that, Jamie was engulfed in a hug from the brother he loved. They clung to each other with eyes shut tight, squeezing to give their angst a safe place to rest in the other's open heart. They had always been a good fit. It was a beautiful thing to watch.

"Brother," Jens whispered. "What happened to you?"

Jamie shook his head. Neither of us were ready to open that can of crap-covered worms. He simply clung to Jens while tears fell down his cheeks and into his beard. It was then I noticed Jamie's beard was clean and less wild. He had bruises, but his body had been freshly bathed and his clothes changed into blue sweatpants and a white t-shirt. So scattered was my brain that it didn't dawn on me until that moment that I had been bathed and was dressed in clothes.

The black yoga pants were baggy on me, and the fitted red T hung off me like it was three sizes too big, but it wasn't scrubs. I wasn't tied down. I'd been given a bit of dignity.

Jens released Jamie to wipe the tears from his eyes. "We have to get you back into bed. You guys can't sleep on the floor." He glanced up at the two beds. "Did you want me to push your beds together? That way you don't have to be separate. You seem to want to be near each other. Would that help everything calm down a little?"

Jamie nodded emphatically, grateful someone seemed to understand.

"Okay, then. Let's get you up." He spoke over his shoulder to the nurse, his voice cracking. "Grace? C-could you help me lift Jamie? I'm afraid he'll break something if I do it wrong." The nurse's wide hips bumped Jens as she neared. I backed away from her advance, but didn't hit her this time when she reached out. Jens and Grace lifted Jamie off the floor and onto his bed. She redid the IV he'd ripped out when he'd toppled onto the carpet, and they adjusted his pillows so he could sit up without putting forth much effort.

Jens approached me slowly, as if I was a wild animal. Honestly, he wasn't too far off. Had I the strength, I would have run away before anyone else could lay a hand on me. I was so turned around, and only medium sure it was the real Jens. "I'm going to push the beds together so you can stay right with Jamie, but to do that, I have to move you.

Would you rather Grace move you instead? Or Elsa? I can call Elsa up if you want."

I looked around the room and realized where we were. We weren't underground. We were in the Huldras' lair. I'd never stayed in this room before, but the décor was similar. Everything was white and beige in their giant home, and this room was no different. White walls, beige carpet, beige comforters. But we'd been outfitted with medical gear scattered about the room to monitor and rehabilitate us.

Jens was waiting for my response, but I wasn't sure. I blinked up at him, and finally motioned for him to come a little closer. When he consented, I got a better look at his features. I'd never seen him with a beard before. It hid half his face from me. I tried to sit up so I could see him better, and he leaned in to accommodate my feeble effort. "Can I help you? I'll just get you to Jamie, and then I'll give you your space, if that's what you want."

His face was so sincere. I studied the bags under his eyes and the earnest way he looked at me – yearning, yet controlled for the greater good. I don't know how long I stared before I finally consented to his offer for help with a slight nod. His hands were slow and purposeful as one snaked around my back and the other looped under my knees. "Am I hurting you? Is this okay?"

I touched his chest, not sure if that served as a proper response or not. Jens laid me beside Jamie, who wrapped his arms around me greedily. Though he knew it was Jens and not a trick, it still felt like we only had each other. Jens pushed my bed over so it touched Jamie's. He rearranged my pillows so I fit in snugly next to his best friend. I watched his cautious movements and intentional care of us.

Jens was always careful with me.

When he slid a pillow under my legs to prop them up, I lifted my hand to clumsily touch his face. As if we were two magnets, Jens sat on the bed next to me, looking deep into my eyes as my hand felt its way along his newly acquired facial hair. It was prickly in parts, but mostly it was soft. I touched the crinkles next to his eyes that accordioned whenever he laughed, though he didn't look like he'd done much joking around as of late. My thumb traced the crest of his cheekbone, trying to recall the thousands of other times I'd indulged in the motion. My thumb found his full lips, and I could feel his eyes on me, watching every breath and movement with trepidation. My lips parted and mouthed his name, and I could tell they weren't as dry as they had been when I was last awake.

Jens exhaled the burdens of his duty in a gust of elation that tickled my face with the scent of warm cookies. "Yes! It's me. Jens." He pressed my hand to his cheek, savoring the contact we'd been barely surviving without. "You're in there. You're still you." His relief was palpable, and I could tell he was holding himself back for my sake to keep from scaring me. His eyes were filled with sincerity and longing. He looked like home, and I'd been without that for too much of my life.

Jens leaned forward slowly, giving me every opportunity to pull away, and rested his cheek to mine. I inhaled the freshly baked sugar cookies he always came with and closed my eyes as his arm wrapped around me, stroking my ribs and separating me from Jamie.

The inch of distance was too much. I began to panic, shaking my head and shrinking back into Jamie's chest.

Jens retracted immediately. "What's wrong? Too much? Did I hurt you? You're so fragile now. I'm sorry, baby. I just... It's been so long without you. I've been searching for months with no sign from you! Where were you?"

Jens was selfless in his love for me. He didn't mind that I needed in my basest of needs to not be parted from his best friend. He overlooked my ragged and deteriorated state and saw the me *I* couldn't even see anymore.

Whatever doubts I'd been harboring retreated under his powerful gaze that was always fixed on me.

It was Jens. I was safe.

18

CRAZY JAMIE

*J*ens eventually passed out on the bed next to me while I slept in Jamie's possessive grip. When Jamie awoke, it was with an animalistic clawing at the IV in his hand again. He ripped it out, chest heaving and eyes wild as he fought to once again make sense of his surroundings.

Poor Jens would never get a full night's sleep with the two of us around. He woke up and talked Jamie down to reason, reminding him that we were safe, and he was real.

But if Jens is real, where's Britta? Jamie asked me, lying back down so I could hold him while he fought with his demons for tranquility.

I mouthed my girlfriend's name to Jens, who nodded. "She's here. She's downstairs. When you're ready, she can't wait to see you both. But you have to get a little better first."

Both Jamie and I grimaced at that reasoning. Why shouldn't Jamie be allowed to see his wife right away? What could possibly keep Britta away from Jamie?

Jens understood my confusion. Jens always understood me. "When you first got here, you attacked me, Foss and Grace a few times. Britt's dying to see you, but we can't have you trying to strangle her. It's just not safe."

Jamie's mouth fell open. I listened to his thoughts that were similar to mine. Neither of us recalled attacking Jens or the others. I didn't even remember seeing Foss except briefly in the car on the way here. Most everything was a blur between reality and our dream life, so it was hard to tell what was actually going on. Jamie closed his mouth and nodded.

Jens called Grace back in to fix Jamie's IV again, and this time Jamie didn't fight her. I could tell he wanted to attack anyone who wore scrubs, but he remained motionless because it got him one step closer to Britta.

Jens laid back down on my other side and stretched his arms toward the headboard. Then he dipped his hand to run it through my hair. The touch caught me off-guard because I hadn't seen it coming, so I flinched and clung harder to Jamie.

"I'm sorry! Man, that really wasn't supposed to scare you." Jens sat up. "I've got to know what happened, guys. Why aren't either of you talking? Worse than that, you two haven't made a single noise the entire time since we found you. What did they do? Grace said there wasn't too much damage to your vocal chords, but the black marks around your neck when we first saw you were like a ring or something. What was it?"

I mimed a collar around my neck and then acted out a dumbed down version of the shock running through my body.

"You got choked?" Jens guessed, his thick eyebrows furrowed. "Someone choked you?"

I shook my head and motioned for him to get me something to write with.

"Duh. Of course. One second." Jens hopped off the bed and came back twenty seconds later, ready for me to write down some concrete answers. Colonel Mustard in the Library with the electrocuting collar.

With the utmost care, Jens helped me to sit up against the headboard so I could write on the spiral notebook he slid across my lap. Jamie was still lying down, but his cheek was pressed to my hip and his arm was wrapped around my thighs as I tried to master the mechanics of properly holding a pen.

I wasn't sure where to start. There really was no beginning anymore.

Jens sensed my confusion and guided me with an even tone. "Let's start with who had you."

That was easy. *Sirens,* I scribbled.

To his credit, Jens only yelled once. "Sirens?! Are you sure? How is that possible?"

I scribbled with untidy, angry letters, not bothering to

anchor my words to the lines on the page. *Tucker drugged and abducted us when we were trying to escape the attack on his Pearl house. He handed us over to a crapload of sirens, which is where we've been. Underground somewhere, imprisoned by the psychotic sirens.*

"Tucker did what?!" Jens grabbed at the paper to make sure he was reading my scrawl correctly.

Jamie was unbalanced. We both were, really, but I only flinched when Jens's hand moved too quickly for my liking to take the notebook from me. Jamie's hand flung out in a claw and tore at Jens's arm like a tiger who had his food snatched at. He clutched me to him, eyes wide with anger that had a note of fear to them.

Jens held his hands up and flipped his legs off the bed, standing so Jamie could see he meant us no harm. "Jamie, it's me." Though he was trying to be understanding of something he couldn't begin to grasp the depths of, the hurt was clear. "Brother, what did they do that you don't trust me?"

Jamie watched his best friend with caution, his cagey glances darting from Jens to the door to the IV in his hand. *They would have given us Britta if it was real. It's not real! It's not Jens!*

I let Jamie's arms tighten around my ribs because he needed the comfort. I motioned for the pen and paper, and Jens handed it over slowly, making sure not to touch me so as not to upset Jamie.

I scribbled out, *Jamie won't believe it's you until he sees*

Britta. The sirens messed us up, but I know it's you now. Then I paused, the doubt flooding me at making such a bold declaration. *It is you, isn't it?*

Jens nodded, softening. "It's me. Who else would I be? And I'll bring Britta up just as soon as Jamie's under control. Brother, you just attacked me. Britta's pregnant. I won't have you doing something you'll regret."

Jamie yelled in my head. *Jens doesn't have a beard! Even when his parents left for Be, he still shaved! It's not Jens!*

I motioned to Jens's beard, which obscured the face I'd grown to love.

Jens scratched his chin. "My beard? Yeah, I haven't shaved in a while. Shoot, I haven't showered in a while." He knelt down at the bedside, careful not to touch either of us so Jamie didn't get spooked again. His hands clasped in supplication. "I haven't done anything that wasn't directly related to getting you back here in months. I only ate to keep myself sharp for the task. Everything, and I still failed. I didn't even find you. You found me. I'd love to hear how that all came about, when you're up for it."

I nodded and wrote, *My mom found you.*

Jens's eyebrows puckered in confusion. "Your mom found me?" Then he closed his eyes, pained at the revelation that I'd finally cracked. "Okay, baby. That's nice."

I didn't bother to correct his assumption that I wasn't nuts and bolts. I probably was permanently beyond what would pass for normal.

Grace knocked lightly twice on the door before letting

herself in. She carried a tray with two bowls on it and a pitcher of water. Jens moved slowly, meeting Jamie's trepidacious gaze as my boyfriend reached forward to help resituate my slumped torso. "I'm just trying to help her up so she can eat, okay? I'm not taking her anywhere, and no one's going to hurt either of you."

I tried to calm Jamie down, but I had precious little assurances for my own self, let alone to spare on him. Everyone breathed with relief when Jamie held his cool as I was straightened against the many pillows that cushioned my aching joints. I felt marginally stronger than the day before. I guessed the IV was giving me back some of the things I'd been lacking. Though the tube scared me, it seemed to be helping, so I gave it the benefit of the doubt.

Jamie's peace only lasted so far. When Grace tried to spoon-feed him some broth from the green ceramic bowl, Jamie snapped. He smacked it out of her hands and shoved her across the room with more force than he'd had a few days ago. He was getting stronger, too, but his lucidity was questionable.

Poor Grace was disheveled, but thankfully, not hurt. It was almost as if she expected this and had braced herself for it. I wondered how much of our haze between fear and comfort had we actually been coherent for.

Don't eat the food! They'll separate us again! We can't disappear from each other, Lucy! We have to get home!

I felt half a step ahead of Jamie, as far as lucidity went, and the difference was Jens. As much as I understood that

Britta couldn't be put in danger, I knew Jamie wouldn't eat or get better until he saw her.

My hand shook from disuse as I gripped the pen again while the nurse and Jens tried to calm Jamie down. He was strong enough to stand, but only just, so they overpowered him gently and sat him down.

Jamie was crazy.

I was crazy.

I shook my head, determined the loony bin would not be my home. I'd waited long enough for a real place to belong to. I wouldn't belong in Crazy Town.

No more, I decided. *No more.*

19

I LOVE IT, AND IT DIES

started writing and didn't stop for as long as my hand stayed with me. A few times I had to drop the pen to drink the broth Jens fed me. I hated, absolutely hated being fed, so I made it my mission to recover as quickly as possible so I wouldn't be in a relationship where I was the mess anymore.

That was easier said than done, but writing everything down was a start. I filled the entire page before my determination began to waver, my grip going lax without my permission.

Jamie had calmed in only the bare minimum of definitions. Each sip of the broth brought a warning from him, but I took the bullet, showing him that even though I ate, we didn't lose each other. Still he clung to me as he laid by my side. His arms were wrapped around my hips as if I was his last gold coin and the bandits would soon come and take me away. I was sitting up in the bed. Well, propped up on a mess of pillows, but I think that still counts.

Jens kept his distance, sitting at the foot of the bed and gently stroking my feet under the blanket as if they were made of the thinnest glass. He was patient, and I was grateful. Every now and then I would look up from my notebook and stare into his longing gaze with just as much desire to be closer to him. Though neither of us said it aloud, we decided to move slowly for Jamie's sake. He was taking much longer to come back to himself.

By the fourth page, the words started to run together. I set the pen and notebook down on my legs, expecting Jens to pick it up so he could piece together our abduction. Jamie surprised us both by taking the notebook and starting his own account. He'd been reading mine as I wrote, and I watched him write, curious to see how different our time apart was.

Jamie's hand was unpracticed, but he managed, scribbling angry strokes of the pen that tore rips into the page.

Chained to the floor in a black cell. Heard Jens's voicemail, and then got a shock. Pain in my arms.

I love it and it dies. I love it and it dies. I love it and it dies. I love it and it dies.

Porridge poisoned. Starved. Taking the bond away. Playing Jens's voicemail with a shock on our legs. Can't move from the chains. Can't stand. Cold floor.

I love it and it dies. I love it and it dies. I love it and it dies. I love it and it dies.

On and on Jamie wrote out the mantra that drove his nightmares. He scribbled until he tore the paper clean in two, breathing heavily through his teeth like an animal.

My hand drifted to his brown hair and stroked the curls there with clumsy fingers, hoping to bring him peace I was wishing for myself.

Britta's dead! Jamie wailed, turning his head and weeping into my hip. *If it was Jens, he would've brought her to us by now! Britta's dead! My baby! My child is dead! I love it and it dies. I love it and it dies.*

I took the pen and paper, flipping to a new page. I asked Jens on paper if Britta was dead.

"What? Of course not! Jamie, no. Britta's fine. She's healthy, still pregnant, and the baby's good as far as the doctor can tell. We're just waiting until you get ahold of yourself. Did you want to maybe try talking on the phone to her?"

I shook my head for Jamie. They'd used our voicemails to torture us. Nothing short of the real thing would suffice. I wrote as much to Jens, who sighed, running his hand over his face.

"Jamie, you have to start believing that I'm not going to hurt you. You're safe now. I'm your brother, and I'm here. Just try a little harder to believe that, and I'll bring her right to you. I can't risk you hurting her. You have to stop attacking your nurse and me, first."

I could hear Jamie's internal debate and knew he was tilting in Jens's favor. I'd drank a whole bowl of broth, and we were still alert and together. We had escaped the sirens. Jamie just needed that one last bit of sanity before he let himself believe the unbelievable.

20

———

CHICKEN AND CARROTS

It took a whole day to get everything I knew about the situation on paper. Jens waited until the end to leaf through it, his face growing grim and sickened with every paragraph he absorbed. Punch after punch landed in his gut, punctuating the pain of his worst fear – that something bad would happen to the few people in his life, and for all his muscles, he would be powerless to stop it.

"Grace!" Jens barked down the hall.

She entered the room with the practiced edge of bracing herself, but this time Jamie did not attack. Oh, the desire was there, but he was controlling it now. His fingers itched to hit her, but instead he held onto the bed and to my arm, breathing deeply through his nose to fend off the urge to fight.

Jens spoke in clipped tones. "I need you to start

treating them for electric shock wounds. And when can they eat solid foods? Lucy's getting smaller by the minute!"

He and Grace went back and forth on different approaches to treatment until Jens was a little less irate. He tore his phone out of his pocket and beckoned the person on the other end to take his place for a few hours.

I thought the sight of Foss would bring me peace or answers or comfort or something, but instead I felt only the same hesitation that kept me from believing Jens was real. When we were locked up, I did my best never to let my mind wander to Foss. Foss was a landmine, and I was already underground.

When Foss entered the room to take Jens's place, he regarded me with the same uncertainty. He could barely look at me, while all I could do was stare blankly at him. I watched every movement for signs of falsity that might indicate the man sitting in the chair across the room was not actually Foss.

"I said stop staring at me like that!" Foss barked, arms folded across his chest.

How long had he been talking? I blinked at him while Jamie postured next to me. He was sitting on the side of the bed, feet on the floor in anticipation of walking. He'd waited for Grace to go make us some food, knowing he'd rather fall than let someone in hospital scrubs come too near him. Jamie rubbed his thigh muscle, doing his best to coax it into usefulness. He was determined to get to Britta.

In his mind, he'd gone without attacking Grace for a couple hours now, so he should be able to see his wife.

"What? I'm not kidding, Lucy. Stop looking at me. I'll leave right now if you don't knock it off." Foss was angry as he stood.

I'd heard him talking, but I couldn't look away. I had to know if he was real. Had I really been married? The whole thing seemed ridiculous. Disjointed. I'd met Foss because of Uncle Rick.

Uncle Rick was dead. Even though my mom used his power in my mind, he was still dead.

That's right, Jamie confirmed. *So if Alrik comes through that door, we know it's not real.*

Okay. Then help me figure this out. I met Foss because I had Pesta's rake. But he was terrible. He... did he push me around?

Yes. He's Fossegrimen.

Why would I marry someone who pushed me around?

Jamie shrugged. *That's a good question. We were on the Isle of Fossegrim. He married you to make sure no one tried to abduct you again.*

I had a ring! I exclaimed, bits and pieces surfacing as if through a muddy puddle. I looked down at my finger, and then recalled the size of the thing. It was built for The Rock, not me. It had hung around my neck. *Did they take it away?* My concern grew when I felt my collarbone and didn't find a ring. Someone had taken my wedding ring. I didn't know much about marriage, but that seemed like a big no-no.

No, Lucy. You got divorced. You gave the ring back to Foss. You're with only Jens now.

That's right. I love Jens. Jens is real. We're not underground. We're together.

Foss was towering over me next to the bed, doing his best to be intimidating. My gaze fell to the ruby on Foss's finger, which was right at eye level to me. He was saying something, but I wasn't listening. I reached out and grabbed the jewel, pulling his hand toward me so I could inspect the ring up close.

The fire. It branded me. I'd pulled Foss out of the burning house. I'd lived there in a red dress. I'd been his wife. We were friends now.

I nodded, pulling on his hand to drag him down to my level. He knelt by the bedside, grousing as he allowed me to examine his fist. "What are you doing?" he asked, wincing each time he looked at me.

My fingers moved to his face, trembling as they touched his cheekbones. I knew so much about him, and yet it felt distant, like I'd lived those choices in a previous life.

Foss closed his eyes so he didn't have to look at me. "You're too thin." He looked pained at having to say it. "You're not you. I don't like it. You used to be... but now you're..." When my finger traced under his chin, he whispered, "What did they do to you?"

I didn't answer. There weren't words, even if I'd had a voice.

A sandy-haired man in blue scrubs came in with a tray of food. This time I wanted to attack him, though not for the same reasons Jamie did. Roasted chicken and carrots wafted toward me, and I forgot all else. I dropped Foss's face and reached for the food like a greedy child. My stomach was empty, and I needed to fill the gaping void inside with something other than questions and lies.

No! It's a trap! It's not Grace! It's poisoned, Lucy! They got you to lower your guard! It's not Foss! It's not Foss! They'll take you away again!

Even if it was true, I wanted the food – needed it, even. But the moment the bowl was placed on my lap, Jamie picked it up and threw it across the room, shattering the green ceramic against the opposite wall. He lunged at the male nurse, but fell, shaking like a madman before the well-trained nurse could force him back on the bed.

Foss whisked me away from Jamie and deposited me on the floor so he could help the nurse pin Jamie to the bed without anyone knocking me over. I took my moment and dragged my legs using my forearms and abs toward the remnants of my meal. I knew I had only seconds before Jamie took my food away again, so I snatched up the nearest bit, which was a thumb-sized chunk of chicken. I brushed away a shard of the plate and tore into the flesh, breathing hard at finally tasting real food. I wanted to weep, but there was no time. I grabbed a carrot and shoved it into my mouth, then another and another. It was all I wanted in life, and I attacked each bite with zeal to rival a wild animal.

Foss let out some noise of distress and scooped me up off the floor. "I'll get you a new plate! Don't eat off the floor! You were a Tribeswoman, and now you're begging for scraps off the ground? No!" He turned to the nurse, his tone authoritative, as it always was. "Jamie's cracked, but I know there are parts of her left in here. I'm taking her downstairs to eat. Jamie's completely mental! She's my wife, so this is my call."

Jamie tore at the nurse's shirt and reached to claw at the man's face at the mention of Foss taking me away. *I knew it would happen! I told you not to eat! Food takes you away from me! No!*

Jamie, we're dying! I have to eat sometime! It's been too long we've been without food. I'm sorry! I have to try!

No, Lucy! Don't leave me in here! They'll shock me again! They'll tie me to the ground. Help!

I turned my face into Foss's shirt and wept for my weakness. I wept for Jamie and my inability to stay strong for him. I wept because I was weak, and I hated myself for the unforgivable state I'd deteriorated to.

21

PEANUT BUTTER AND CHEESE

"How does that feel? Is the stretch too deep?" Jens asked of my wince. My knee was atop his shoulder with my foot dangling over his back. His face was inches from mine as he helped me with my four times daily physical therapy regimen. The deep stretches were painful, but what was worse was that I had my boyfriend literally between my legs, and there was zip chemistry between us. He was kind and gentle, which should have been wonderful, but it felt awful. I was the sick person, and he was the caregiver. I hated it. He hadn't done more than peck my forehead in a week. When he would leave, I did my exercises by myself to cram in some extra credit. I hated this phase and wished to move past it as soon as humanly possible. I wanted to be back to where we were closer to equals. "Baby, you have to answer me," Jens reminded me patiently.

Oh, yeah. I was so in my head these days, it was hard to remember to interact with people who were not Jamie. I shook my head in response. Not that it mattered. Jens stopped taking me at my word last week when I'd indicated I could walk on my own and ended up falling and banging my chin on the table.

He dropped my right leg and picked up the left, hooking my knee over his shoulder and leaning in to give me a good stretch. "Am I hurting you?"

I tried not to sigh as I shook my head. He was so careful with me. It was sweet, but I felt like his senile grandmother. I remembered being able to banter and bicker with him in our flirty way, but that fire seemed gone. We slept together at night, but I was so afraid of the dark that I made him bring in a night light. Jamie had the same anxiety, once our eyes began to adjust to normal light again. Jamie slept with a lamp on, waking up every few hours to make sure he wasn't in the dark anymore.

"Lucy, you have to try concentrating when I'm talking, okay?" Jens wasn't even upset that I had no idea he'd been speaking. We were suddenly stretching my back, and I hadn't noticed the switch.

My eyes found his, and I was overcome with desperation to be in the moment – any moment. Jamie had been inconsolable for the entire week after Foss took me out of the room, and still he called for me when his fear and confusion grew too great. Parts of him knew we were safe, but the fear was sometimes more real than logic.

Charles Mace and Linus were in my imagination as I tried to make sense of all the questions surrounding them. Linus came over to me with his hands shoved in his pockets. *Lots of drama over there with the new emo sibling,* he commented. *What's up with you?*

You're not real, I told him. *Go back to Mace and hang out.*

That's mean, Linus huffed. *I would never tell you you're not real. I feel real. How about this?* Linus reached out and pinched my arm. *Did you feel that?*

I batted his hand away. *No. I told you. You're not real. Go away.*

Dang it. I thought you would've made me real by now. Linus shoved his hands back in his jeans pockets and went back to Mace, casting me forlorn looks at having to endure making friends with the loner who wasn't all that chatty.

I turned back to reality, only to find myself in an empty room. Jens was gone, and I wasn't sure how long I'd been alone.

The urge to break down was always there just beneath the surface, but I didn't want that. There had been enough holding me back. I sat up and flopped my feet onto the floor, testing out their commitment before sending them into action. I'd walked down the hall plenty of times, but they'd all been with Jens or one of the nurses as a crutch. I wanted freedom. I wanted to go outside. I wasn't even sure what month it was anymore. I had to shake the voices in my head, and figured fresh air was the way to go about that.

I wasn't as terribly thin as I had been when they'd rescued me, but I had a long way to go. I compensated by eating like a horse everything they brought to me, but my joints were still stiff when I put pressure on them.

I shuffled my feet to the door, loving the thrill of going somewhere by myself. I was determined not to fall down, so I held onto the wall as I padded down the carpeted hallway toward the stairs. They'd put me on the second floor, and the steps down to my goal greeted me like they were as ominous as climbing up a mountain, as opposed to, well, walking down thirteen stairs. I tried not to get discouraged at the waif I'd been reduced to. Just a few months ago I'd been rock climbing and kayaking, building muscle and holding my own.

Just a few more months, and we'll be back to normal. Good as new, Jamie assured me. *You're doing well. Go slow.* Jamie had been pacing his room for some time now, attempting a round of pushups and taking my example of working extra hard to rehabilitate his body.

I made it down the steps and leaned on the wall to make my way to the kitchen. My eyes appreciated the evening far more than daytime, but even midday, my retinas could mostly handle the aggravation. I meandered into the kitchen, searching through the cupboards for something fatty with lots of protein. I despised feeling so weak, and was determined to get my curves back as soon as possible.

I pulled down the jar of peanut butter and a loaf of

bread, and then raided the fridge, finding only some cheese that looked appetizing and was filled with the required fat. I sat down on the stool at the counter and made myself a peanut butter and cheddar cheese sandwich with feeble fingers.

That's going to make us sick, Jamie commented, though I could feel him salivating.

You want me to make you one?

I… no. That's gross. I waited five seconds for his obligatory consideration, and he pushed out at me, *Well, if you feel like making another and you find you can't finish it, I wouldn't be opposed.*

Will do. I'll make you two. It's actually pretty good. I smiled as I chewed. *You sound better tonight. More like you.*

I need to see Britta. Convince Jens I'm ready.

I scoffed. *I'm halfway to nine kinds of crazy. My word doesn't mean a whole lot. Just keep calm and try not to attack anyone. Eat what they bring you.*

Jamie's response came back in a small voice. *I'll eat if you bring the food to me. Otherwise I'm afraid it'll be poisoned.*

My heart broke for Jamie and all he'd been through. *Of course I'll make your food and bring it to you.*

A panicked Jens shouted through the house, "Where is she? Lucy! Lucy!"

I wanted to answer, but my voice was uncooperative. Instead I banged on the counter three times.

A freshly showered and shaved Jens tore down the stairs, knife out like a wild man. His eyes were wide as his head whipped in my direction. "You... are you okay? How did you get down here? The nurses know not to move you without discussing it with me!"

I offered him a smile and a bite of my sandwich.

He tucked his knife back into his bootstrap and made his way to my side. "You made yourself a sandwich? You came down here by yourself to make a sandwich?" I could tell he wanted to scold me, but he caught himself. "Is it good?"

I held the coveted sandwich close, shaking my head with a slight tease.

He pulled my chin toward him with a smirk I hadn't seen in ages, looking over my face as if searching for something. "There it is. There's that moxie. You lost it there for a while, but I knew no one could take it away for good." Then, just to spite me, he leaned over and took a giant bite of my sandwich. His cocky grin mutated into a grimace a few chews in. "Ack! What is that? That's disgusting! Is that peanut butter and cheese? Like, cheese and peanut butter?"

I nodded, laughing silently from my stool as he spat it out in the sink and washed his mouth out under the faucet. That was worth all the work it took to get down the stairs. I loved Jens when his personality was in full swing. He'd been careful with me, gentlemanly and subdued. I'd hated it.

"You put like, half the jar of peanut butter on there! And why the cheese? What, was the jar of tartar sauce empty? So gross! And you think I'm a freak for liking orange circus peanuts." He shuddered. "Ugh. I can still taste it."

My smile touched my eyes, and for the first time in months, I felt a positive shift. So much of my personality had been based in silliness; being without jokes and shtick for so long felt wrong. I gazed up at Jens, wondering how on earth I'd survived without him.

Jens paused his tirade on my awesome sandwich to look me over, taking in the small change. "You're smiling. It looks like you again. I've missed that."

I motioned him over so I could get a good look at the face that had been hidden beneath a beard for far too long. When he plopped down on the stool next to me, I began to appreciate how giant he actually was. Six and a half feet tall and ripped with hulking muscles built for tearing apart trolls, Wereunicorns and the like, Jens was intimidatingly handsome. I reached over and traced one of the veins running the length of his bicep, smirking at his shiver. He caught my hand, scrutinizing me for signs of lucidity before he made his move.

I didn't feel like waiting. What can I say? There's something about a garden gnome in a tight black t-shirt that makes a girl ask for what she wants. I slammed the mental door on Jamie, fisted Jens's shirt and pulled him close, laying one on him as forcefully as I could. I didn't have much strength in me, but Jens humored me, which I appreciated.

I kissed him, long and passionately, relishing in the taste of lust I'd been barely surviving without. I didn't want to be the sick person, and began to understand why Linus got pissed off when I was too nice to him when he was recovering. I wanted to be strong and sexy, to rival him in a verbal takedown and brag that he could never keep up with my sense of adventure. I wanted more than a sick room and grandfatherly pecks on the forehead. I wanted lips and tongue and fists and hair-grabbing.

Jens was lost in the moment, and for that stretch of time, we were the only two sharing a fire that started from a single fledgling spark. He wasn't aggressive, but he let me pull and grab at will, moaning with surprise and satiation as he sunk into me, eyes closed as I tugged on his lower lip.

When my stool began to tip backwards, I grabbed tighter to him, and the kiss slowed to a stop before Jens knocked us both over. "Who knew you had *that* in you?" he breathed, placing the last vestiges of the explosive kiss on my lips. "Most days, you can barely hold a conversation. You're feeling better, I take it?"

I nodded, pulling him in for another round. I didn't have much energy, but my body rallied for Jens.

We were interrupted by a conversation making its way to us, so Jens pulled back, running his hands over his messy black hair as if mussed tresses were a dead giveaway of passion in the kitchen.

"He wasn't there. I'm telling you, you've never gone on a manhunt with a Huldra before. If he'd been at any of the places on the list, we would've found him." It was Elsa, the leader of this Huldra coven who I alternated between hating and being cool with. I hadn't seen her since before the mess, so I didn't know what to make of her anymore. She stopped short when she rounded the corner with Leif and Foss, and saw me not holed up in my room like a recluse. "Well, if it isn't my favorite *Domslut*. Little Lucy in the flesh. How is it you're up and about?"

I picked up my sandwich to show her what I'd been up to, taking a bite as I blinked up at her.

"I thought I'd like you better silent, but this is testing my patience. Leif, could you at least teach her some more sign language? It's been too long."

Leif nodded and stood on the other side of the counter, his friendly smile too genuine to be frustrated with. He walked me through the basics I'd already caught on to, having hung around him. Plus, I'd taken a semester of sign language at one of the high schools I'd been to.

I participated in the lesson mostly for Jens. He was paying close attention to everything Leif did, treating the signs as if it was the only way he could communicate with me. We'd been doing just fine before Elsa'd shown up, but whatever.

When Leif grasped my aptitude and Jens started asking for repeats and slowing down, I got up to make Jamie a couple sandwiches. I could feel Foss watching me. He gave me a wide berth, as did Leif and Elsa, as if they were afraid of breaking me if they got too close.

I was determined not to be useless. I made Jamie two sandwiches, and a second one for me, though I couldn't even visualize choking it down. I signed to Leif, asking if they had sealed bottled water. I knew Jamie wouldn't risk anything else.

"I'll buy you that pink unicorn you've always wanted if you can actually eat all those sandwiches," Jens challenged me, leaning his elbows on the counter. "On second thought, don't. I think Grace would quit if she had to clean up puke on top of everything else we've put her through."

I signed that they were for Jamie, which made Leif give me a slow applause to commend my efforts. Jamie had been pretty difficult for them.

Jens went with me up the steps, carrying the tray and letting me lean on his elbow without any disparaging comments about how winded the small bit of exercise made me. Jamie's room had been bolted three times from the outside with a barricade of a chair against the knob, as well. Jens moved the chair and unlocked the door while I warned Jamie I was coming in with Jens.

Jamie was standing in the corner, fists at the ready in case... I'm not sure what he was expecting, but he let his arms drop when he saw me. Jamie stared at me with wild eyes and even crazier hair. Then he pounced. He didn't mean to jump out at me so frantically, I'm sure, but I hadn't been allowed to see him in a week.

Jens intercepted Jamie, putting his hand to his friend's

chest to calm the bull. "I know you want to see her, and you can, but you have to be gentle."

The moment Jamie calmed down, Jens lowered his guard, and Jamie engulfed me in his arms. *You're okay? No one's keeping you locked up?*

No, but I've been cooperating, which is more than I can say for you. I made you some lunch.

Thanks! I'm so hungry, but I don't trust the food.

I snuggled into his burly chest. *It's alright. I'm here. I won't let anyone poison us. We really are safe, Jamie. Eat something.*

Jamie plopped down on the bed and dug into the sandwiches I'd made, rolling his eyes at the comfort the simple meal delivered. He yanked me down next to him, making sure he had one hand affixed to me wherever he went.

"You gotta know how frustrating it is that you two are talking to each other, but not to any of us," Jens huffed, taking a seat on the only chair in the room. "If you could try to include other people, it'd make me feel a little better."

Tucker, Jamie thought to me as he chewed. *We have to find Tucker and end him before he gets to us again.*

I signed Tucker's name to Jens, and then pounded my fist into my palm, making my message of vindication clear.

Jens sighed. "Believe me, I'm trying. I want to find Tuck just as much as you two. He has to answer for his part in all of it. But I've tried all his usual haunts, and he's nowhere. And everyone thinks he's dead, so no one's any help in finding him." He leaned back in the chair, trying to look relaxed, but I knew his planning face well. "There's one other place he might be, but it's too far away for me to feel comfortable leaving you two. Once you get back on your feet, I'll go and finish it." There was a shadow of shame that crossed over his face, and I regretted that Jens had to do the dirty work of disposing of his old friend.

Jamie pounded his fist to his chest and shook his head. *I'll do it.*

Jens pushed enough of a smile onto his face to lighten the mood. "No. This is my job. Lucy's my charge, so I neutralize the threats concerning her. Love the enthusiasm, brother, but you're not ready to fight anyone. Focus on getting better."

Jamie glowered at Jens as he shoved the rest of the sandwich in his mouth. He picked up the second without thought of the taste. He was beginning to adopt my mantra of eat anything in sight to regain the weight and do whatever it took to get on with life.

22

TOO MUCH CHEESE

As the days passed, my mission was united with Jamie's only inasmuch as I needed Linus's ashes back (or his soul, if you wanted to get technical). I hadn't explained my plan to Jens; he was still under the impression that my mom in my mind had been imagined. Though he couldn't explain how we'd busted out of the lair, he couldn't place his belief in dead people communicating with the living.

He clearly hadn't seen as many slasher movies about hauntings as I had.

I stirred the eggs in the pan, adding extra cheese so Jamie would eat a healthy helping. We'd been doing much better in the week since Jamie had let me bring food to him. We'd been lifting weights together, doing calisthenics and had even progressed to slow jogs around the massive property the Huldras owned. Jamie hadn't attacked anyone in over a week, and had earned the right to see his wife again.

Britta sat at the counter, her fingers worrying the hem of her snug purple shirt as she waited for the eggs to be finished. Jamie was still asleep, otherwise I knew he'd be busting out of his room to get his hands on his wife.

Britta was a cute pregnant woman. Her athletic build lent itself to her carrying the baby with little other changes to her body thus far. Though I'd spent an hour with her that morning, I couldn't stop staring. I mean, girlfriend had barely peed on a stick last I'd seen her, and now she had the beginnings of a small, round swell and that pinch-your-cheeks glow about her.

"That's too much cheese," Jens said, critiquing my cooking, as usual. He was such a control freak. It made me want to add more cheese just to show him his meddling didn't do anything to change my mind.

That's how Jamie likes it, I signed, bumping him with my hip to get out of my way.

He stepped his leg in front of me and edged me out with his butt. I swatted at his stellar backside, but it did little to move him. I huffed and watched as he added herbs that simply made the eggs far too busy to be comforting. As much as Jens was trying to annoy me, and kind of was, it felt good that he wasn't afraid to touch me anymore. I was starting to look a little more like myself, though I knew I still had a ways to go. Britta hadn't seen me except for that first night they'd found us, and her mournful eyes followed me wherever I went.

I missed you, too, I signed to her, changing her pity to a warm smile.

"I hated staying away when you needed me. Are you well? You look..."

I wrapped my arms around her neck and pecked her cheek. I would get better. Pretty soon, it would be as if none of this ever happened. I was determined.

When Jens finished with the omelet, I threw a fistful of cheese on top of it just to spite him. I grinned at his protesting groan. "Oh, come on! I had it perfect."

It didn't matter how Jamie liked his omelet, really. Once he got an eyeful of Britta, he wouldn't care about anything else.

Britta held her brother's hand as they followed me up the steps. Two knocks on the door roused my buddy from the bed. I made sure to keep my thoughts to myself when I strolled into the room, knowing that he should eat at least a few bites before his heart exploded all over creation. *Hurry and eat. I've got a surprise for you, big brother.*

Jamie wolfed down half the omelet in one go. *Thanks, syster. Did you use a whole brick of cheese on this? It's... you're a very good cook.* His grimace told me he didn't care for my cooking, but was trying to be kind. It was the one time I was grateful we weren't speaking. Jens wouldn't know he'd been right.

I flicked his ear as I stood and opened the door, letting

Jamie get an eyeful of the most beautiful woman he'd ever seen. His fork clattered to the plate, and as I'd predicted, the rest of the omelet was forgotten. I scooped up the plate as Jamie ran to Britta, kissing her with passion I could feel through our bond. I swooned as Jamie tried to tame the frenzy inside of him and only bless her face with gentle touches. I left the room with Jens as Britta sobbed with her husband at their long-awaited reunion.

Jens and I went to my room for what he thought would be a simple hang-out while we worked-out. Now that Jamie was back on his feet, it was time to move forward. I sat on the bed next to my boyfriend, loving how well we fit next to each other.

I pulled out a piece of paper and pen from the night-stand and set to work. I scribbled, "Tucker?" on the page and handed it to Jens.

"I can go look for him in a few days, once I know Jamie's under control around Britt."

I nodded, and then set to work explaining my mom's last words to me before the hole in the brick wall was filled back in. Tucker ganked my vial that contained the ashes of my family, along with my twin brother's soul. I told Jens where the body was buried and what we needed to do to get Linus back.

When I finished, Jens read over the rant, his face falling with every line. He closed his eyes and crumpled up the page, pressing the wad to his forehead. "I thought you were getting so much better. I didn't realize you were still...

It's okay. I'll talk to Grace. See what she can do to help you."

I leaped off the bed when he tried to leave to find the nurse, moving between him and the door to block his exit. *I'm not crazy! It's real! It's real!*

"I know, honey. It's alright. Sure. It's real. It's all real." He smoothed my hair out of my face and kissed my forehead in that patronizing sick patient way I wanted to punch him for.

I don't care if you believe me! I'll take Jamie and do it myself!

"Slow down. You know I can't speak sign as fast as you can. Write it down."

I scribbled my message and underlined it twice to show I was doubly serious. My mother had been clear. Linus could live again, and I wouldn't let that opportunity pass. I would fight anyone and anything to get my brother back, including Jens, if it came to that.

"Whoa. You're not going anywhere. And Jamie won't leave Britta just like that. He only just got her back. Your mom died, sweetie. Two years ago, your mom and dad tried convincing the Mouthpiece to save Linus in exchange for their lives, and Pesta reneged. Your mother was taken into Be, and your dad was used to build part of a portal for the humans to enter Be through. Linus died, Loos. Linus is dead." He swallowed hard as he looked deep into my eyes. "Any of this ringing a bell?"

My growl was silent, but effective. Jens backed away

from the door with his hands up. *I know all that! She put her —*

"I really can't understand what you're saying! Please write it down."

I huffed, wishing for Leif. It took five whole minutes, but I wrote down the entirety of everything my mom relayed to me, and how she'd gotten us out of the sirens' lair. I'd already told him she'd busted us out, but he hadn't believed me before.

Jens's shoulders were weighted as he read my account. "You have to know how nuts this sounds. What do you expect me to do with this?"

I wrote in bold letters, *If you love me at all, you'll take me to Tucker. You'll get my necklace back and take me to Nøkken. If I'm wrong, you can put me on whatever pills Grace's got up her sleeve. I promise you, I'm not crazy.*

Jens reached out and held my hand, bringing my gloved fingers to his lips for a kiss that was laced with sadness. "Okay, baby. Okay."

I knew that tone. He didn't believe me.

I didn't much care.

23

TUCKER'S CONFESSION

It was another two days of trying to mute out Jamie's honeymooning with Britta before I convinced him we needed to move. While Jamie had been in and out of lucidity during my mom's instructions, he knew we needed to find Tucker before he tried kidnapping us again, so he was on board with at least part one of the plan.

Foss packed up the SUV without complaining and was silent during the first hour of the ride. He didn't like looking at me anymore, now that I was too thin. I didn't blame him, but I didn't care, either.

Foss and Jens took turns driving and sleeping through the night and on till the evening of the next day, stopping only to refuel and stretch our legs. Poor Britta was uncomfortable, but she didn't make one disparaging comment. I made a mental note to book her a massage when this was all over.

By the time Jens turned off the freeway and down a few winding and poorly lit side streets, he had bags under his eyes and looked more exhausted than irritable. I was wired. I wanted my brother back, like, two years ago, and every day that ticked by without having him annoy me by singing *Safety Dance* felt like a waste of my life.

Jens took a swig of water after he parked the car in the street. He dumped a little over his head to wake himself up. "This is the only place I can think he'd come back to, and he might not even be here, so everyone be cool." He shook his head like a dog, flinging water droplets onto Foss, who'd been given the permanent shotgun seat due to his gigantor height. "Britta, I want you to stay here, but move to the driver's seat. If we need to bust out fast, you're driving the getaway car."

Britta's voice answered with an edge of steel to it. "I can fight, you know. Just because I'm pregnant doesn't mean I'm useless. Tucker did this to me as much as he did this to you, Jens."

Jens closed his eyes and leaned his head back, sighing as he looked at the moon. "I've been driving all friggin' day and night. Come if you want. I don't care enough to fight about it. Vanish Lucy for me and keep her and Jamie out of the way. If Tuck wants to abduct them again, I don't want him knowing they're there if we can help it."

Foss pulled out his machete from under the seat. "Why not just keep all three of them in the car?"

Because we deserve to know why he did this to us, I explained.

Foss huffed. "You know I don't know what you're saying when you do that. Why hasn't your nurse fixed your voice yet? Never thought I'd miss your yammering, but it's a far sight better than you waving your hands at me all the time or writing on your notebook."

I gave Foss the finger – a hand gesture understood by most communities, so there would be no confusion.

"Fine. Come if you need to, but keep quiet." The lateness of the evening and too many hours in the car were getting to Foss, because he laughed aloud at his own attempt at humor. "Get it? You can't talk. Of course you'd be quiet." He slapped his knee as he snorted, and I fought the urge to smack him.

Jens pulled his gun out of the glove compartment. "Alright, kids. Let's do this."

I leaned forward from my place on the middle bench and covered the gun with my hand, shaking my head. *You've been driving too long. Not wise.*

Jens considered this and nodded with regret. "I don't like going in without it, though. Tuck's fast. If he feels like porting, he'll be gone before we can do anything."

I took the weapon from Jens, double-checked the safety and shoved it down the back of my pants, letting it rest on the small of my back. *I'll shoot him if he needs shoot-*

ing. You're too tired to make that call. Plus, I need to be able to defend myself if he tries anything again.

It was a tribute to Jens's exhaustion that he didn't argue further. He dug into his red bag and pulled out an old key, looking on the brass thing with something resembling remorse mingled with fond reminiscing.

Jamie clapped his hands once to get everyone's attention, holding up a paper that read, "No one kills Tucker until Lucy gets her necklace back."

Foss was bored with all the rules, so he got out of the car, shutting his door quietly. I used my small handful of seconds to take as many precautionary measures with the gun as I could, knowing how quickly things could go south if I wasn't the adult in the heated situation.

Britta held my hand and Jamie's as we walked behind Jens toward an old apartment building down the street. Out of the three streetlights, only one was functional. There were several cars parked that were missing a wheel, missing a mirror or even a whole window. Loud music blasted from a barely standing house to our left, though it was well past three in the morning. It was your typical low-income neighborhood I'd been well familiar with in my family's travels around the nation.

We approached the three-story apartment building that looked barely inhabitable. It was a slum fit for rats, but certainly not humans. I wondered why Jens had a key.

Jens motioned for Foss to fall back as he led us up the stairs, and for all their animosity, the two actually worked pretty well together. Jens shoved the key into the lock at the end of the hallway on the left, and opened the creaking door slowly, knife drawn. Jens disappeared inside, and Britta led us in behind him, with Foss waiting in the hallway for signs of an altercation to make his move. Cigar-bogged air bashed me in the face, and I had to cover my nose and mouth to keep from choking on the thick fog that was well past the occasional patio cigar. No, this stank of days, if not weeks of lighting one after the other, relying only on the fact that the windows were too thin for insulation to ventilate the small space.

A solitary lamp was on, shedding light on the only occupant in the one-bedroom apartment that had seen better days, and hopefully, better wallpaper than the mustard and brown polka-dot design that looked sickly and stained.

Tucker St. James's dark hair conflicted with the seventies-style faded yellow wall motif, but the sallow tinge to his skin wasn't too far off. With his cocky smirk nowhere in sight beneath his overgrowth of facial hair, Tucker looked up from his cigar with too much sadness to calculate in a single word. "So you've come," he said simply. "Get on with it, then." He took another puff, flinging ashes into an overflowing glass vase that had certainly not been meant for such tarnishing. Tucker wore his signature fitted pants he'd left unbuttoned at the waist, his usually crisp tailored shirt was wrinkled, stained and looked like it hadn't seen a washing machine in a week. He was barefoot, with his suspenders hanging down over the arms of the mustard and brown floral-patterned overstuffed chair, his too-long legs flopped open in a surrender to his long life.

Jens's resolve was cracking at having to do the terrible deed of offing a trusted friend. "You stole them from me and handed them over to sirens who tortured and almost killed them. I've got every right to end you."

At this, Tucker blinked with a flicker of life that made his voice crack with emotion. "Almost? I've been trying to get into the lair for months. The last time I tried, I ported in without a problem and found myself right in the middle of a watery mass grave. I assumed Jamie and Lucy had died with the sirens. No idea what killed them, though." He put out his cigar, adding it to the overwhelming pile of butts in the vase. "They're alive? Have you seen them to confirm it?" He stood, despite the threat of Jens's drawn knife. He stumbled forward, and I got a waft of strong Gar coming off him. "Tell me I didn't kill them!"

Jens took a step back, but kept his knife up. "Why do you want them dead? Did Johannes send you?"

Tucker regained enough of his personality to scoff. "That Tonttu jackal doesn't have enough gold in all his hills to buy me off. I don't wish them dead. Jamie's your brother, and Lucy... Well, she's more than you can handle, but I wouldn't take her away from you."

Jens lunged so quickly, I scarcely saw the whole movement. He slashed at Tucker's arm, drawing a clean slice across his bicep. "That's a lie! From the second I told you I had a girlfriend, you were all over her! Don't think I didn't hear your subtle flirting she cringed at. Don't think I didn't see you checking her out when she wasn't looking." Jens shouted, despite the open door, punching his chest with his free hand. "I'm *always* looking! I see everything that comes near her, so don't tell me for one second you didn't try to take her away! I know how you work. The shiny new thing turns you down, and she's your next infatuation until you conquer!"

Tucker cupped his wound but didn't raise a hand to fight back. "I didn't understand, or maybe I did. But I didn't want her for myself! I wanted my friend back! The real you, not the housewife version! I heard you talking about your garden. Your *garden*! Planting tomatoes and parsnips like a common garden gnome. You were meant for more than that! I admit, I thought she was holding you back and gladly tried to wedge myself between you two so you could get some perspective, but I don't care about that anymore!" He looked deranged as he lunged for Jens, gripping his friend by the collar with bloody fingers. Jens was too stunned to stab again, having never seen his BFF so out of control. Spittle flew from Tucker's lips as he spoke inches from Jens's face. "When I got used to you two and got to know her, I stopped trying to break you two up. I was even a little happy for you! I swear! I didn't know they'd do what they did. Lucy told me she wouldn't seal the deal with you because of the laplanding bond. I was trying to do you a solid! I didn't know! I didn't know! They said they could fix it!"

Jamie, Jens and I were completely confused. Jens pushed Tucker back onto his sofa chair. "Who said they could fix what?" He readied his knife again that still had some of Tucker's blood dripping from the tip. "And I don't need you to help me get laid! I promised her dad I'd do whatever I could to make sure she stayed a virgin till she got married. The laplanding had nothing to do with that!"

I cocked my eyebrow at the blast of news I hadn't been privy to. Sure, no dad wants his daughter sleeping around, but that dad and Jens had this arrangement threw me completely. I wasn't sure how I felt about it.

Tucker shook his head, holding the injury on his arm with such a sincere expression of sorrow, I almost softened. "The sirens! I was only trying to help you and Lucy. The sirens said they could break the laplanding bond! After what Jamie did to her when he was poisoned, I thought it was the only way she could actually be with you. Sweet girl, honest! I like her, and only wanted to help her! They said they could help her!"

"How did you even know about them? The sirens were supposed to have been killed off!"

Tucker hung his head, his voice catching with emotion as he tried to get out his plea. When he looked back up at Jens, tears were streaming down his angular cheeks. "I helped many of the sirens escape the massacre twenty-five years ago. A couple Huldras and I had an underground lair built so they could live. No one knew that their powers wouldn't work on the Other Side. This world's still filled with pissed off Undrans that might recognize them! They begged me for help, Jens. I couldn't kill them! They were helpless and hunted! It was wrong what Undraland did to them! Murdering a whole race because they couldn't be controlled? All they had to do was banish them to the Other Side, like the Huldras, and all would have been fine!"

"What? They can't control people with their voices on this side?" I'd forgotten to mention that detail to Jens. "Why isn't that widely known?"

"The sirens themselves didn't know until they fled to the Other Side. Then they were stuck here, obvious marks to the Huldras. The Huldras were pissed that they'd also been kicked out because of the sirens, and knew what they all looked like." He swiped at his tears, smearing a line of blood over his cheek. "What was I supposed to do? They didn't deserve to die. Pesta did, but most sirens didn't do anything, Jens. You were a kid back then. If it'd been your call, I'd bet all my fortunes you'd have done the same thing."

"I could've helped you," Jens whispered. "You should have just told me what you wanted to do with Jamie and Lucy. I wouldn't have killed the sirens for just existing."

Tucker laughed humorlessly. "I couldn't have known that. You're living with the *Domslut*! She's a known siren killer!"

"And you sent her straight into their lair without any protection, without consulting her Tomten. You stole her and ran! There's no forgiveness for that!"

"I know!" Tucker shouted. "That's why I haven't asked for any. They took Jamie and Lucy and shut their charmed walls on me. The walls *I'd* charmed for them to keep Undrans from entering without invitation! I was going mad trying to find them!"

"And in the whole mess, it never occurred to you to tell me any of this? Months! I was out of my mind for nearly three months! Do you know what they did to them? They electrocuted them, kept them in pitch black cells for months! Starved them! Mental torture! All to break the bond? Bull! They're cracked, the whole lot of them! Can't control something with their voice, so they try to break it apart, bit by bit! Well, they sure broke her alright! And Jamie? Raving lunatic! Didn't even know who I was! You took what was left of my life and crushed it!"

Tucker dropped to his knees in front of Jens, hands pressed together in supplication as sweat stained his shirt. "Do what you have to. I won't fight back or ask for mercy. Just know that I was trying to fix your life, Jens. I was trying to help Lucy."

"You should have told me! And if you thought you couldn't, you should have come to me the second things went sideways!"

"I knew I couldn't come back to you without her! Come on, Jens! You know you would've killed me on the spot if I didn't get her back first. That's why I've been here at our in between place for weeks, waiting for you to come and avenge her. I thought she was dead!"

Jens's blade trembled, but he didn't lower it, instead keeping it poised above the nape of Tucker's neck. "She nearly was dead when we found them."

Tucker's tears fell fast now as he sucked in what he most likely assumed would be his last breath. "There's no forgiveness for what I've done, but I am sorry, Jens." His hands shook as he laced them behind his neck and hung his head. "End it."

24

SENTENCING TUCKER

Foss had grown in many ways. He didn't push me around anymore. He understood (vaguely) the difference between an employee and a slave. Heck, he'd even gone so far as to make Britta tea to be nice. But I knew my former husband, which was why when Jens hesitated and I heard Foss barge into the room, I wasn't all that surprised.

Britta was, though. She jumped and accidentally dropped my hand, revealing me to the woeful Tucker.

Foss yanked the gun from under my shirt, cocked it and aimed at the fire elf's head. "Sorry does nothing."

Then he pulled the trigger.

Britta screamed and Jens shouted, and I could hear Jamie's outcry in my mind. But I knew a little something Foss didn't. While I knew him like the back of my hand, he hadn't taken the time to really know me. The bullets were safe in my jeans pockets, where they would stay.

Again and again he squeezed the trigger until he grew frustrated and pulled out his machete.

I ran and threw myself in between Foss and Tucker, shielding the unworthy foe with my body. I couldn't overpower Foss, but I could make him pause.

"Move!" he bellowed, and for a second, I wondered if I'd overestimated how much I actually meant to him.

Stop! Just wait a minute.

Jens lowered his knife. "Stop, Foss. This isn't the way. It doesn't do anything." He shook his head. "I won't have Tucker be the first elf to die of stupidity. If what he says is true, he didn't mean for this to happen to them."

Foss was incredulous. "I don't care if he meant for this to happen! It happened! You may not care what he does to your girlfriend, but no one abducts a Tribeswoman and lives to brag about it! This fool dies tonight. If not by your hands, then by mine. He stole from me every bit as much as he stole from you. I bought Lucy. She's my wife in Undraland still. My property. Tucker stole my property, so I have every right to end him. This is how you deal with thieves, Jens!"

Yes, it was a very good thing the gun wasn't loaded and in my hand. I didn't have stellar self-control when those words rained down on me like fire.

Jens postured, and in that moment, I saw the power struggle they were locked in, even though I'd taken myself out of the war by choosing to be solely with Jens. "Well, we're not in Undraland, are we? Lucy's not your property, and she's definitely not your wife here! So back off!"

Foss fumed, spitting on the floor. "A man who doesn't protect his household doesn't deserve to have one."

Jens rubbed his eyebrow, his head spinning. "Let me think it through first. Killing him does nothing. There's no post to hang his head on when you're done to send a message, Foss. Everyone already thinks Tucker's dead."

"It's not about just that! He's a danger to her, and you know it!"

Jens held up his hand to shut Foss up. "Give me a minute to think." He put the butt of his knife to his temple as his eyebrows scrunched together in contemplation. "It's not up to me or you. Jamie and Lucy are the ones who get to decide what to do with Tucker. They're the ones he kidnapped. It can't be about me or you. It has to be about them."

Crap. I knew I didn't want Foss to slaughter him in cold blood, but I didn't have a better solution. Tucker was dangerous when left unchecked. He deserved punishment for what he'd done.

But I needed an elf to do some hocus pocus ninja action when we found Linus's body. Mom said to get an elf to perform a bonding charm once I poured Linus's soul back into his body.

Yeah, I heard it. I know it sounds crazy.

I looked to Jens and pointed to the spot on my clavicle where my Linus necklace used to rest. First things first.

"Oh, right." Jens addressed Tucker. "Where's Lucy's necklace? You took it from her when you abducted and drugged my girl."

Tucker nodded slowly, reaching down into his pocket and pulling out the thing that made me breathe a little easier. I snatched it from him and fastened it around my neck in the next second. I'd been parted from Linus for too long.

Britta dropped Jamie's hand, and he walked over to me, his face grave. *I know you need Linus back, but there are thousands of elves who could help.*

Sure. It doesn't have to be Tucker. But this doesn't feel right, Jamie.

He sighed. *I know. But we can't just let him go, either. He's partly responsible.*

Sure, but he was trying to bust us out after the sirens went crazy on us. That counts for something.

Something, but not everything. Jamie's mind flitted from option to option, considering things for two seconds at a time that I didn't understand the entirety of. *I don't understand why you're fighting so hard to keep Tucker alive. Everyone already assumes he's dead. There's no life for him to return to here.*

It's not for him, it's for Jens. Don't you think he's lost enough? Tucker's one of his closest friends. I can't take that away from Jens. Could you? I can't ask Jens to kill his friend. I swallowed hard. *I had to kill Tonya's body, and I'm not sure I'll ever forgive myself for it.*

Jamie hugged me. *It wasn't Tonya, syster. You killed the Mouthpiece, not Tonya.*

I know, but this really is *Tucker. I don't want Jens to live with this for the rest of his life.*

Jamie and I looked over at Jens with a fond protectiveness, who returned our stares inquisitively, brushing his shirt off as if we were noticing a stain. "It's rude when you two do that, you know, but whatever. One day when you two get your voices back, I don't want any more of this psychic talking stuff."

Yeah, Jens is dreamy, I said, my silly sarcasm finding its way to the surface in the grim apartment. *But he won't be okay if he has to kill his friend. Tucker should live, but you're right, he can't go unchecked. He's too powerful to be allowed to make reckless decisions like that. We should get him a house-plant to take care of. Get him some actual responsibility to tie him to reality.*

Jamie closed his eyes, his expression that of Linus being presented with a salad full of tomatoes. He pulled me tighter into the hug, resting his chin atop my head. *Do you know that I love you?*

Of course. I love you, too, big brother.

He exhaled his discontent into my curls and nodded. *I'm doing this for Jens and for you, just for the record. I don't actually need this.*

Doing what? Did you think of something?

I took part of you when we laplanded that Jens will never have. I can never give it back to him, but I can do this for him. I can keep Tucker alive and make him useful, grounded, so Jens doesn't have to lose another person he loves.

Jamie released me and motioned for a pen and paper, which Britta produced by rummaging around in a few drawers in the bedroom. Jamie scribbled out, *Can you perform a bonding charm?* and showed the paper to the despondent Tucker.

"What? Yes. Of course I can."

Jamie nodded and wrote out two more simple sentences that set loose a mic-drop of epic proportions to everyone else, but made little sense to me. Gasps sounded all around the room as Jens read aloud, "'If Britta's okay with it, Tucker can either choose to die or he can be my *vakt*. I don't care which.'"

25

VAKT

After about ten minutes of everyone going bonkers with arguing and questioning and basically acting like children, I gave up trying to understand what they were talking about and flopped on the smelly sofa chair. Tucker's hands were still clasped behind his neck, though his eyes were far away and deep in thought as he remained on his knees.

Though I'd been working my way up to being actually physically fit, I was nowhere near it. The small exertion of standing for so long and enduring the emotional nonsense was taxing. Despite the chair's cigar stink, I curled up in it, bringing my knees to my chest and staring blandly at the drawn blinds. I wanted Indian food – buckets of the stuff. I wanted a bed that wasn't at the Huldras and hadn't been burned to the ground. Tucker was the man who destroyed my life while trying to save it. Through my childhood and now into adulthood, his flapping cape left a trail of wreck-age. I resented him, and in many ways had a healthy fear of the damage he could do with a cool smile on his face. But underneath the monster mask, I could see the error of it all. The error of my hatred and misdirected fear. Though part of me wished him dead, I knew I couldn't pull the trig-ger. Heck, I couldn't even give Foss the bullets so he could pull the trigger.

Whatever a *vakt* was, it was decided the offer would be put to Tucker to choose between death and doing what-ever the other thing entailed. Tucker looked up to Jamie's kneecaps and nodded. "I'll take the oath tonight, if you can procure the tools."

Foss was not mollified. "This won't be like how it is with Jens. You're Jamie's slave until you've repaid the debt you owe him. That's whatever a prince's life is worth, you chewed up piece of garbage. Then you can be a proper *vakt*."

Jens glowered at Foss. "I don't know what you've been smoking, but *vakts* aren't slaves. It's our choice to protect, not our job to shine shoes and make beds and whatnot."

Jamie held up his hand to Foss and shook his head. The prince had lived on his own amongst his people without slaves; I couldn't imagine him being cool with things changing so abruptly.

Foss huffed. "Fine. You nearly got my wife killed. You'll be her slave until I say otherwise. Then you can live out your days as Jamie's *vakt,* keeping her safe through their bond while you look out for Jamie. Maybe by then you'll have learned a little bit about your place in the world. How to act without endangering the thing you're trying to help. Useless."

Tucker looked up at Jens from his spot on the floor on all fours with a mournful expression. "Please don't make me do this. You know I'm best on my own. I was meant for more than guard duty. I didn't mean for any of this to blow up like it did. You have to believe me."

Jens crossed his arms over his chest, his knife pressed against his massive bicep. "I believe you, but this is the second time you've almost killed my girlfriend. And there's no shame in being a *vakt*. I'm not beneath you, Tuck. My job has just as much honor and prestige as yours. But nice to know how you've really felt about me all these years."

"I didn't mean it like that." Tucker grimaced. "I'm an elf, though. My life will far outlast Jamie's. Your life sentence is nothing compared to what you're asking me to do!"

Jens nodded, glancing toward Jamie, who rolled his eyes and waved his hand to give Jens the green light to make whatever deal was necessary for the situation. "Fair point. You can take your oath for a normal lifetime, then. After sixty more years passes, you're free to seduce old ladies and be as stupid as you'd like."

Tucker hung his head, weighing the pros and cons of dying on the spot versus six decades of being useful.

Britta was fed up with the stalling. Her knife glinted

against the lamplight. "I don't care how you mean it or how you feel about doing real work instead of playing with matches as you please. *Vakt* or die. I don't care which. But I won't go to sleep tonight wondering if you'll put my husband in danger another day. Choose now, or my knife will choose for you." It was clear by Britta's grip on the hilt what her choice would be for the playboy who was four times her age.

What the crap is a vakt, Jamie? I asked, growing weary of no one talking to me, yet making decisions that would directly affect me.

Oh! I'm sorry, syster. Jens is a guardian gnome, so he's a Tomten vakt. An elf who takes the same vow of guardianship for a family is called an elfin vakt. Same thing, just different races.

I thought personal guards were only Tomten.

No. They can be any race, really. They're just not all that common anymore. I put it out there that Tucker should be mine. Then we can keep an eye on him, and it would mean extra protection for us and the baby.

I sighed. *Okay. But then we're saddled with Tuck for the rest of eternity. He's kind of more trouble than he's worth, in my opinion. His help is dangerous.*

That's him helping unchecked. The vow ensures he'll act in protection of our family. He scratched the back of his neck. *At the rate we're going, that might not be a terrible idea.*

I closed my eyes and exhaled, trying to play the part of a reasonable adult when what I really wanted to do was run. Oh, how I dreamed of running away from all of them.

I wanted to snatch up Jens's hand and bolt for the nearest airplane, never looking back.

Linus. I had to find Linus first, and then the three of us could run.

If only.

Thanks a lot, Jamie grumbled. *Nice to know you'd ditch us if we didn't have the bond.*

I didn't bother excusing my thoughts, but instead shut the door between our shared psyche so I could indulge in a moment of private dreaming.

26

A NEW START

Jens returned from his trip to who knows where of gathering all the things he needed to turn Tucker into a sensible adult who cared about the welfare of others. It was no surprise to me that this great feat required magic.

Foss had his long machete trained on the kneeling elf in case he tried any funny business. It was making me jumpy, and I wished the whole thing could just be done with.

There was little to help with, as Jens, Jamie and Britta were the ones most familiar with the process. They set about making what looked like a potion and smelled like rotting chicken and eggs in the kitchen on the stove. I knew it shouldn't, but the stench reminded me that I should be eating like a linebacker if I wanted to get healthier. I nudged Foss's machete out of the way and tapped

Tucker on the shoulder, miming eating something when he turned to look at me.

"What?"

I repeated the motion, hoping it wasn't too rude I was asking to raid his cupboards.

"You're hungry? There isn't much here, but you can order whatever you like. Phone's in the kitchen."

I glanced up at Foss with a silent request he use his voice to order takeout for us. He responded with a frustrated huff. "Fine. What do you want?"

I shrugged, not knowing how to sign "Chinese food" without just finger spelling for him, which he wouldn't be able to understand. I mouthed for him to pick whatever.

"Look, slave," Foss growled at Tucker, "you move a muscle, and I'll hear about it. Don't make me use this." He pushed his machete through the sheath on his belt and left for the kitchen.

"You're awfully quiet," Tucker commented when it was just the two of us in the quaint living room's lamplight.

I nodded, pointing to my throat.

"Why aren't you talking?"

I really had no way to act this out that would make sense to Tucker, so I got up and retrieved Jamie's pen and paper, scrawling as briefly as I could the incident with the collar and the shock therapy, plus the burning honey-like substance they'd used in the beginning to burn our throats and render us mute.

The paper fell from Tucker's trembling fingers. "They did what?"

I touched my throat in response.

"Lucy, I'm so sorry. I had no idea they would take such a brutal route. They said they could help, so I assumed it would be, I don't know, old roots they had growing underground or something." His shame-filled gaze could barely look at me, but he kept his eyes on my neck as if in study. "I might be able to help speed along the healing."

I recoiled from him, drawing my feet up to my chest to get away from his dangerous brand of "help".

Tucker nodded, turning back away from me. "I understand. It's just a few simple herbs and a *reparerande* charm. You'd probably be talking again in a few minutes. I won't know the extent of the damage unless I can feel the area, but I can't imagine it'll heal on its own any time soon."

I crossed my arms over my chest and looked out the window, doing my best to ignore him. While I didn't wish him dead for Jens's sake, I didn't want him in my business, either.

The others came out with their concoction of liquid gag in a mug, somber faces all around. This was a big deal, a ceremonial permanence that was being done in secret to a dead man.

Tucker rose slowly, wary of Foss's violent swings, and took the blue "If it's not emptied, don't talk to me yet" mug. He looked into the chunky, smelly slop with the saddest expression I'd ever seen on the cocky man. "I could've ported, you know. I could've left instead of making this choice. I hope you see that I'm not running from my responsibility, from what I did."

Jens crossed his arms over his chest. "You know if you did try to hide, I'd find you. There's no running from the damage you did. Now drink your medicine."

Tucker postured, finally looking Jens in the eye. "Fine, but I'm no one's slave. I'll repay my sins by protecting Jamie and his family, but I'll not be talked down to like a servant. I'm choosing this instead of running or dying. It's a great service I'm doing him, and I won't have that overlooked."

Foss opened his mouth to argue, but Jamie held up his hand, earning the silence he demanded. He met Tucker's eye and nodded, his mouth drawn in a tight line. He extended his hand to Tucker, and the two shook as equals, and without grudges or anger just waiting to be unleashed on the other.

"And to this end, I swear it." Tucker took a centering breath before downing the entire contents of the mug with his eyes closed. No sooner had he swallowed the last drop did his body start trembling. He dropped the mug to the floor, and as the ceramic shattered, his knees clacked together.

I was caught by surprise when Tucker's legs gave out, but Jens was not. He caught his old friend and lowered him gently to the ground away from the mug's shards. He grabbed a thin book from the wobbly end table and shoved the hard spine into Tucker's mouth as the man's teeth began to chatter violently. Though I'd experienced a seizure (thanks to Elsa and Tucker), I'd not seen one play out at my feet. The others backed up, but I couldn't just sit around and watch the mayhem. I dropped to the floor and held Tucker's left arm down while Jens manned the right side and his head, which thrashed around like a vibrating ball. Tucker's muffled howling scared me, though I tried not to let it show.

Jens called over his shoulder, "Jamie, take Lucy and go outside!"

Jamie didn't need to be told twice, but I sure as smack did. I shook my head, unable to leave someone who was writhing around like he was being dowsed in acid.

It was my laplanded buddy who extracted me from the mayhem and gently pushed me out into the hallway. His hand was tight over mine as he set about explaining the way of the world to me. *This is all normal, but it's about to get ugly in there.*

I scoffed. *Like I'm afraid of ugly. Stop little woman-ing me. Tucker's really hurting!*

Jamie was serene through my criticism. *Jens is in charge, and he doesn't want you there for this. You have to respect the leader. Don't you trust Jens yet?*

I... Well, he... I had no coherent retort, only spluttering. *Don't you know me yet?*

Tucker's shouts turned into screams, and then mutated

to choking as what sounded like gurgling blocked his windpipe.

He can't breathe! I cried, trying to push Jamie aside so I could get back in there. I knew the Heimlich and CPR.

Jamie's arms went around me in a hug that was nothing like affectionate. He was restraining me, and I despised that I was still weak enough that I couldn't overpower him. He braced himself against my thrashing and dragged me in my hug down the hall. *This is all part of taking the vow! He's fine. If he survives, it means he's worthy of the task, and the pain will pass.*

I was floored. *If? If?!* Tucker was howling, and as much as I was still mad at him, I didn't believe in torture – especially after having experienced it myself. *You'll kill him!*

Then he was meant to die! Don't you see? If he lives, we know we can trust him. If he dies, well, then Jens didn't have to sully his knife with his friend's blood. Jamie dragged me down the stairs as I fought him, skidding my feet on the soiled carpet to slow him down.

"Jamie!" Britta protested, running after us. "Jamie, put her down! You have to get in there to revive Tucker when his heart stops!"

Alarms were going off in my head, and I protested harder. *You're going to kill him!*

Britta followed us outside. "I can watch her. Go on up, or this whole mess will have been for nothing."

Jamie nodded after releasing me with a stern look and a warning to stay away.

I signed to Britta that I needed to be back up there, but she shook her head. "I'm so sorry, Lucy, but you can't. Tucker will be fine. He chose the *vakt*, so he'll be able to transition without a problem. We just have to be patient." She pointed up the street. "Walk with me. When Jens went through the process, it took several hours of suffering I wish I'd never witnessed." She had a haunted look in her eyes. "Tucker will be fine."

I internally rolled my eyes as we walked together down the dark litter-lined street. I knew how to at least spy on the guys. I tiptoed up to the door in my mind and gently pried it open, peeking through the crack to see what Jamie was watching.

Instantly, I regretted my actions.

Tucker's legs were kicking out as a scraping cry of agony erupted from the poor man on the floor. "Ah! It's burning! It's acid on my insides!"

He fought free of Jens and tore off his shirt, howling in a way I knew I'd never forget. Tucker looked down, drawing my eyes to his bare torso. Underneath his skin, I saw terrifying little finger-sized lumps running up and down his body, like fast-moving slugs in his veins pumping. They raced as they lit his skin with agony Tucker could only scream incoherently about. They were sprinting, going up his stomach, along his throat and into his cheek, where they gathered like a town meeting. His poor cheek swelled until it looked like Tucker was sucking on a whole orange on one side of this mouth.

"You're doing great. Breathe through the pain!" Jens instructed his friend, though the angst in his voice didn't lend itself to much confidence in the offered comfort. I knew that forced reassurance well.

"Lucy, haven't you been listening?" Britta's voice held a note of scolding to it.

I turned to her, apologetic, but not sure why she expected I wouldn't use the bond to sneak a peek. I plopped my butt down on the side of the street, watching the worst alien torture movie unfold before my mental eyes.

I didn't move for twenty minutes, but watched with tears in my eyes as there seemed to be no end to Tucker's desperate pleas for deliverance. Three-inch rips were cutting through his skin from the inside now. As soon as blood started to ooze out, the skin repaired itself, like doing up a zipper. The number of skin zippers grew, until I counted fifty at a time peppering his body, opening up and closing like a flower over and over again. Each rip open brought about a fresh wave of agony for Tucker, who yelled to the ceiling through the entire ordeal, well past the point of coherence.

"He passed the test," Foss declared. "He'll live. Jamie, come finish the ritual."

The bubble in Tucker's cheek began to throb like a heartbeat, moving in and out as the elf writhed and twitched like he was being jabbed with an invisible poker. With each push out, the mass left a pink imprint that began to take shape. At first it was a wonky circle, then three circles tied in loops. Then a small detailed diamond shape, not unlike the one Jens had tattooed on his face, began painting itself on Tucker's cheek.

Jamie's hands were pressed to Tucker's chest, and he began murmuring in a language I didn't know, a spell I'd never heard of. I wondered if my parents had done this to Jens.

There was a tug of agony from Tucker's lips, and then the little subcutaneous slugs began to dissipate, travelling back down his body and returning from whence they came.

It felt like a solid five minutes of Tucker going through yet another ferocious seizure. When he finally went limp with a pathetic whimper, I shot up off the curb and motioned for Britta that we were clear to go back inside. Poor girl. I'd been horrible company this entire time.

I bolted up the stairs and burst into the room, running to Jamie as he knelt next to Tucker. I moved Jamie aside and scooped Tucker's wide shoulders off the ground. I held his head to my chest, burying my face in his sweat-laced hair. *That was horrible!* I cried to Jamie. *How could you let him go through that? He could've died!*

He's alright. It's what Jens went through for your family, only Jens's was far worse. Lasted nearly an hour. Tucker only swore a portion of his life to me. Jens swore his whole life to your family. I won't begin to describe the horrors Jens went through for you.

Before Jamie could shove down the memory, I caught an image of Jens writhing on the ground in a similar fashion with his back arched and body bent in a rainbow of pain. Then Britta was holding her brother, who had soiled himself in the throes of the torment and lay unconscious and drooling in her arms as she sobbed. A man in a dark cloak performed the same ritual Jamie just had on Tucker, and I realized without even being able to see the man's face, that it was my dad. I knew him in the same way you could know the sun was rising even if you had your eyes closed. Britta and Jamie had been in the same room with the amazing Rolf Kincaid, though it looked like no verbal exchanges had been made.

I shuddered and gripped Jens's arm with my free hand, not knowing how to communicate how not worth that experience I was.

Jens shrugged off my sincerity, lest it become infectious, and went to get Tucker a glass of water.

I rocked the too-tall man in my arms, squeezing him tight so he would know he wasn't alone. Though Jamie had only been there psychically to hold me in the cell, it had made all the difference. While I didn't forgive Tucker for everything he'd done, it wasn't in my makeup to stand back and watch while someone suffered. Call me naïve. I don't really care.

Tucker shuddered a few times against me, letting out the last of his sobs into my bosom, wetting my shirt. When he finally regained the use of his arms that had been exhausted from the tremors, he reached over and gripped my upper arm, squeezing with a pathetic grasp to communicate his gratitude that I had come back to him.

I pushed his hair from his forehead with my free hand as I rocked back and forth, allowing him the space to break down at the pain and the loss of his lifestyle of untethered freedom. Though seducing Pearl, Gladys and who know who else wasn't my idea of awesome, I could relate to the small choices you treasured being yanked away from you for the "greater good".

When Tucker was finally strong enough to sit up, Jens was ready with the water. I watched as Tucker sagged against his friend like a child, wincing as his throat constricted.

The buzzer rang, and Foss paid the delivery kid for the five pizzas and plopped them on the table. I kissed Tucker's temple and then Jens's lips before following the scent of olives and pineapple into the kitchen. Britta and I polished off two pieces each before the guys joined us. Jamie and Jens had helped Tucker to his bed and sat with grim faces at the table as they devoured half a pizza each before coming up for air.

We were silent, no one wanting to break the solemn mood from witnessing the ceremony I'm guessing not many got to see. I wasn't the only one with drooping shoulders and eyelids. Despite the magic of the night, we were all exhausted. Jamie swallowed the last bite of his seventh slice of pizza, and then went with Britta into Jens's old bedroom. It was strange that Jens had once shared an apartment with Tucker, but judging from the shabbiness and the general lack of care, it didn't seem like those were cozy and happy times.

Jens knew I needed the lamp on to sleep, so he left it on for me. Being in the dark gave Jamie and I extreme bouts of anxiety, due to our imprisonment.

Jens fished around in the closet and pulled out all the old blankets they owned, spreading them on the ground for the three of us to share. Though I had slept many times sandwiched between the two men I loved, it was the first time the arrangement felt wrong. No longer did I feel that connection to Foss that made me instantly confused and guilty. Our affair was a distant memory, wiped into clarity by my incarceration. I waited until Foss and Jens laid down before I shifted into place on the outside of the two at Jens's side.

Foss sat up in confusion, but knew he could say nothing as to why his friend's girlfriend wouldn't snuggle him through the night. The line had been drawn, for better or worse.

Jens took in my tired face with a hesitation that dampened down his eternal relief that I wouldn't keep the dysfunction going for the rest of our lives. *Thank you,* he mouthed.

I pressed a silent kiss to his lips and burrowed into his warmth as he brought the blanket up around us. *I'm sorry it took so long. I love you.*

Jens nodded and rested on his back, staring up at the ceiling as he breathed for what seemed like the first time in a while.

I knew that I'd done that to him. The man had gone through physical torture to promise himself to my family, and I'd made him hold his breath so I could be selfish and indecisive. When I'd been starved and broken, Foss could barely look at me, while Jens scarcely left my side. I was a selfish wind elf, a thoughtless water elf, a calloused Huldra, a hurtful siren and the worst kind of human.

And yet, I realized as I watched his thick eyelashes close while he drifted off to sleep, Jens loved me.

27

TALAR HONUNG ELIXIR

Tucker was gone when we awoke, but Jens assured me that was the norm. He was an autonomous creature not used to having to be accountable to others, so letting us know where he'd disappeared to would take him some getting used to.

Foss had gone to pick up breakfast for everyone, and my stomach rumbled in anticipation of the omelets and croissants I would soon gorge myself on.

Jens was different when everyone began to meander about the house and make small talk to pass the time before heavy planning mode set it. He no longer felt the need to play it cool and give me some space. If my hand was out of my pocket, he was holding it. If my hair was down, he was touching it. He wasn't Romeo all over me or anything. It was the little nuances that took our relation-ship to a level of seriousness I had not anticipated my mere act of only sleeping with him would set in motion. Nothing else had changed, but I guess I had, and so had he.

Foss returned with a hard look on his face and a breakfast of fast food ham and egg sandwiches, bagels, juice, pancakes and hash browns for everyone. Jens and I ate quietly, his hand affixed around my waist, and mine resting on his thigh.

Tucker ported back to us, landing in the living room far more alert and his old cocky self than he had been when last we'd seen him. He had an armful of bags that he brought into the kitchen and laid out on what little was left of the drab countertop. "Good morning, children," Tucker sang as he picked up a sprig of dried herbs and hoisted up a massive dead toad by its flipper from out of the bag. "I trust you saved me some breakfast?"

When no one responded, I started assembling a plate of food for Tucker and placed it next to his mystery bags. "Thank you, darling. What a nice little housewife thing to do for your big man."

My expression mutated into a glower. *So, we're back to that, are we?* I picked up his toad and dropped it onto his food, bumping him hard with my shoulder as I made my way back to Jens to finish my meal.

There was a toad, seven different sprigs of herbs, a handful of dirt, a cup of unmarked liquid and a small envelope of green powder that Tucker poured with all the care of using dynamite.

"What are you making?" Jens asked around a mouthful

of pancake. Foss kept a close eye on Tucker, but remained silent with his scowl in place.

After a minute of blending, the entire kitchen smelled of earth and stale gym socks. Britta blanched, and I felt bad for the poor pregnant woman with a heightened sense of smell.

"Anyone thirsty?" Tucker inquired. "No? Just Lucy and Jamie? Well, alright. More for them, I guess."

Jamie and I shook our heads as if they were attached to the same string.

Tucker poured the concoction into two tall glasses and set them on the table, a proud expression beaming on his impish man face. "Drink up, kids. A toast to your new superhero." He slid his hand over his left suspender as he straightened.

Jens stretched out his arm between us and the glasses. "What are you up to?"

Tucker leaned back against the counter, his arms crossed over his chest in self-satisfaction. "That there's a *talar honung* elixir. You're welcome." He bowed his head slightly, accepting our silence as applause. When we didn't drink the nastiness, he prodded with, "I personally don't need to hear the sound of your girlfriend's chattering, but I thought you might, Jens."

I frowned and pushed the glass away, not willing to put something in my body from Tucker – especially when I didn't know what it was.

"It's supposed to... what? Bring back their voices? What's in it?"

"Oh, I forgot one thing." Tucker put his hands over the cups. As he exhaled, tiny tongues of fire dripped down from his hands almost like honey, heating the drinks and changing the color to a sickly pinkish gray. I was surprised the glass didn't shatter. The smell mutated from gym socks to a burnt rubber stink.

Britta ran from the kitchen to vomit in the bathroom, and Jamie followed after her to hold back her hair like a true gentleman. He deserved a kid. Not just a regular kid, but like, a crazy smart one with dimples and riddles and buckets of cuteness.

I shook my head at Tucker, who harrumphed dramatically. "You say you want me to guard Jamie, to be his *vakt*, but you scoff at my help?" He tsked Jens, who sat back to indulge in the familiar back and forth with the friend he'd missed. "I thought all that nastiness was behind us by now."

Jens chuckled, as if the whole thing was cute. "Oh, Tuck, it's almost sweet you think I'll let you give my charge an unmarked drink. You've only been responsible for someone else for a few hours. You'll learn." He scratched his scalp and shrugged at me. "Maybe we should've started him out watching a goldfish."

Tucker pointed to the elaborately etched gold circle and diamond design on his cheek. "If Jamie dies, I die. I'm not stupid. If there's anything I'll protect, it's myself. So Jamie just became the most well-guarded man on earth."

My head jerked from Tucker to Jens, begging for an explanation. Jens glowered at Tucker. "That's not her business to worry about."

I scoffed and started signing angrily about the idiocy of that statement.

Jens rubbed his hand over his tattoo, tired of the conversation before it properly started. "It's no big deal, Loos. It's part of the swearing in every guardian gnome has to go through. It's a whole big thing. Could we not get into it right now?"

Jens didn't need to know sign language to understand the rant I was replying.

"How can you not have told her about your vow?" Foss confronted Jens. "You're telling us she has no idea your life is tied to hers? No wonder she's so reckless."

"It's nothing to get worked up about." Jens tilted his head back and addressed the ceiling to escape taking in whatever my response might be. "If I die, you're fine. You'll be unprotected, but otherwise fine. Since you're the last person in your family, I'm linked to you. If you die, my life's tied to yours, so I'd, you know, stop living too. No big deal."

I had no words, even if I could talk. It was a thing of fortune, actually. It saved me from having to apologize for the cussing out that might've occurred if I'd had a voice. In lieu of yelling at him how terrible he'd been to keep something that huge from me, I slammed my fist on the table. We would have words about this. Many unladylike words.

Tucker brought us back to the present. "It's not poison, Jens. Try it if you don't trust me. It'll give them back their voice." He eyed me with that playful sleaziness that made me want to smack him across the face. "Though, I can understand the show you're putting up. It'll keep your woman quiet longer. Every man's dream – a silent little beauty." He held up his hands in mock concern. "No, Lucy! Don't drink the thing that'll make you better! It's poisonous! You shutting up for another few months is for your own good!"

Jens shoved the drink toward Tucker. "Show me it's harmless."

Tucker sighed. "Really? After I just drank the tonic of death last night? Fine." He picked up the cup and pinched the bridge of his nose, downing a dainty sip and smacking his lips in mock satisfaction. "Good to the last drop." He sat the cup down in front of me, leaning his fist on the tabletop. He towered over the table and looked down at me. "It's a simple potion, darling. Drink up, or get used to keeping your mouth shut while you wait it out."

I debated downing the stinky drink. I hated being silent when I had a mission burning inside me. Linus was buried, and I needed to get his soul back to him now. I wanted my brother back, and knew the quest would require me to be able to talk on occasion to make my way through Undraland.

Foss rolled his eyes at my obvious internal debate and shoved Tucker out of the way as he took his plate to the couch. "Don't even think about touching that, Lucy." He took a giant bite of his food and muttered, "If she murders Jens for being a permissive idiot, I've got dibs on his knives."

I rested my elbows on the table and leaned my head in my hands, sighing in frustration at the decision that had too many pros and cons to list. I knocked on the door to Jamie's mind, but he kept it shut tight.

Jamie stormed out of the bathroom and stomped into the kitchen. He picked up his glass and glared at Tucker. Before anyone could stop him, Jamie downed half the glass in one go, choking and gagging through the last of the liquid until it was gone.

Jamie! This affects both of us! You can't just drink things from dangerous people like it's nothing! It's my life you're taking that bet with!

Tucker smirked at the prince's discomfort and pointed to the second glass. "One of you has to drink the other cup, too. I split it up because it seemed unfair to force one of you to drink the whole thing. I've had it before. Horror of an aftertaste. I'd wager Britta's more kissable than you are right now."

That was the wrong thing to say. Jamie flew around the table, cuffed Tucker on the back of his neck and shoved his head down on the table.

Porting was a useful tool, but I was never prepared for

it. Tucker vanished before Jamie could take his full anger out, reappearing on the couch next to Foss. "Your little group is a touch high-strung." He stretched his arm behind the sour-faced man, who scooted over to get some space from Tucker's smarmy expression that didn't need a woman around to appear sleazy.

Jamie snatched up the other glass and poured the liquid down his throat, gripping the table with his free hand as he muscled through his gag reflex.

I threw up my hands in exasperation. *Fine! Do whatever you feel like. I'm just along for the ride.* I stood abruptly as my stomach churned. I pushed out my chair from the table and flung my hair over my shoulder in the best huff I could muster. I stomped into the living room and walked out the front door, slamming it shut behind me.

MAKING BABIES IN THE ALLEY

I knew I wouldn't make it far before someone came after me. I couldn't get a lick of space from the group, though for months all I craved was someone to stay with me in the darkness.

Jens came trotting down the steps behind me. "Loos, come on. I didn't lie to you. I just didn't want you to have to worry about something like keeping me alive. Don't be like this."

I whirled on him, my finger in his face. *Don't you follow me!* I said with my eyes.

"This is a hole of a neighborhood! You can't go wandering off whenever you feel like having a childish tantrum."

I reared back. "Childish?" At the sound of my own voice escaping my lips, I touched my mouth and whimpered with relief. "It worked?"

Jens gusted out his elation, his shoulders loosening. "That's awesome! What a relief! I didn't want to have to pound on Tuck. You want some water?" he asked as I coughed, my voice raspy and hoarse from disuse, but not nearly as bad as one might expect. It merely felt like I'd been sucking on cotton balls, not as though I hadn't uttered a sound in months.

I shook my head, recalling my indignation. "No, I'm still mad at you."

Jens rolled his eyes at my anger. "Go ahead and use your first words in months to yell at me over something that isn't even my fault. I didn't make the rules of the vow, Loos. That's just how it is across the board."

I gestured wildly with my hands as I spoke, forgetting that I didn't need to use sign language anymore. "We're supposed to be equals, and you're still keeping things from me! It never ends with you! Just when I think I know you, the bottom drops out and there's a whole mess of crap beneath it. Why are you always hiding from me?"

He bit back, incredulous at my gall. "Why? Because I want you to be happy! And you're one to talk. You're secretive too, Loos. Do you think it's easy being in love with you?" He started gesticulating wildly with his hands, matching my level of frustration. "Everything's so tied and linked and bonded and laplanded around you – I have to tread lightly. Do you think I want to put *more* stress on you? If I'm doing my job of keeping you alive, it's not something you'll ever have to worry about."

"You still should have told me!"

"What would that have done?"

My hands fused to my hips. "It would have made you not lie to me! Are you serious with this? What else are you hiding 'for my own good'?"

Jens licked his lips. "Nothing. That's all, and it was just so you didn't have to worry. Your life's already linked to Jamie's. I won't put more on you like that if I can help it."

"You're still bent on hiding things from me, then! You make me crazy!" I shot at him.

"Well, you *are* crazy!" he fired back.

We stared at each other, steaming and stewing and clenching our fists at our sides as we gritted our teeth in matched frustration.

I'm not totally sure when we started kissing. I was certainly in no mood and knew I didn't look any variation of sexy at the moment. It was a mutual attack that led us to the alley between our building and the slum next to it. It was the dirtiest place I'd ever made out in (I hope). I slammed Jens back against the brick, kissing him with all the anger I had in me. Our lips fought as mutual moans and growls escaped us. The passion built to a frenzy, and I found myself backed up to a dumpster as Jens pressed my hands to the metal above my head. I shut the mental door that led to Jamie, knowing he could feel the heat building in my body.

Jens was the best kisser. Of all his talents, I'm glad I knew that one well, and exploited it at every available opportunity. My knees went weak as our tongues tied us together, and soon I was lying on the ground in the alley, my legs wrapped around his waist as he kissed me for all he was worth. I'm pretty sure my back was fighting the ground for space with a balled-up napkin and an old takeout bag, but my brains were pretty much on a tropical beach vacation by that point, rolling around in the warm sand with my hot boyfriend.

Then, just as out of nowhere as it started, Jens began to beg off from the kiss, slowing to a stop as he panted above me. "What just happened? What was that?"

"That was you saying you're sorry for hiding things from me," I explained, nipping his lower lip. "And being a total jackfish."

His eyes rolled back in pleasure as he indulged us in another few minutes of gentle kisses to replace the attacking ones we'd barely surfaced from. "I don't think so, Mox. I think that was you apologizing for yelling at me, and then thanking me for keeping you safe all these years."

"I do love you," I admitted. "And thanks for keeping me safe. But don't hide things from me anymore."

He didn't agree, but his answering kiss scrambled my brains enough to stem my stored-up arguments. His pelvis pressed into mine, and I stopped caring about too many things all at once. After all the chaos that ripped at my life, there was only Jens, and he was such a beautiful thing.

He kissed me once more, his breaths long and heady. "We should... not in the alley. You're going to get tetanus."

I watched him pull away so I could sit up, and like a gentleman, he brushed the filthy napkin and who knows what else off my back. I felt awkward, but elated at the same time. That's the thing about losing your head to a really good kiss.

29

SPEAKING UP

I was so unused to the exercise of talking that I was afraid my volume was off whenever I opened my mouth.

"What? Speak up, babe." Jens was leaning back in his chair, his arm slung across the back of my chair as we all sat or stood around the kitchen table.

"I'm just saying that whoever wants to come with me can come. I'm going either way. I don't much care who believes me and who thinks I'm insane. Linus is my brother. If there's even a small chance I could get him back, I'll be jumping on the next train that'll take me straight to that shot in the dark."

Foss ran his hand down his face, exasperated with either me or the late hour, it was anybody's guess. "Let me get this straight. Your dead mom placed her spirit inside you behind a wall, where she stashes all your Undran abilities? Then she somehow got the most vindictive siren ever to make a fair trade of her life for preserving Linus's soul? You've had his soul on you this entire time in your necklace, but now you need to go back to Nøkken and stuff his soul back in his body to bring him back to life?" Foss stared at me, his black eyes not withholding his clear opinion. "That sounds totally logical. Remind me again why we're letting the one who's clearly had her brains messed with make any kind of decision here?"

"I'm not crazy!" I shouted, disproving my point.

Foss's pacifying tone made me murderous. "No. I hear dead people telling me to dig up other dead people all the time." He turned to Jens. "You're not actually considering this, are you?"

Jens folded his fingers over his toned stomach. "I don't know what to believe, but I know better than to go against Mox when her family's on the line. At worst, we'll go there and Linus won't be buried in Nøkken. It's a pretty specific spot Hilda told her to look for. Linus was my friend. I'd do the same for any of you. If there was a chance to raise back Nik, Tor, Alrik or --" He stopped short, and we all knew he wished he hadn't almost brought up Charles Mace. Jens swallowed. "I'd take that chance for Linus."

The loss of Charles stabbed me in the heart, renewing my fervor in my quest for Linus. I would have one brother back, so help me. "He's there. I'm sure of it."

Foss was incredulous, clearly wishing I was still mute. He slapped his palm to his chest, his volume causing me to flinch. "I'm dead in Undraland! I can't just go walking around the countryside like it's nothing. And Jamie's family tried to have him killed or turned insane so they could dethrone him. You really think it's wise to go traipsing around Undraland with that kind of mark on us?" His eyes trailed to Britta, who remained affixed to her husband. "I made the mistake of travelling with two women before; I'll not be saddled with a pregnant one."

Tucker was leaning against the counter, stroking his left suspender slowly as he took in the tenor of the back and forth. "Is it widely known that Lucy and Jamie are laplanded over there?"

"I don't think so," Jamie answered. "We didn't lapland until we got to the Warf, and we kept it pretty well hidden. We were good in Nøkken and Fossegrim."

Jens spoke up, his finger in the air to pause us. "Stina knows, and she was in cahoots with Jeneve, so it's safe to assume Tonttu might be in the know."

"Didn't you use the laplanding card in Elvage when they threw me in jail with, you know... with Mace?" My throat went dry as I tried to shove down the things that they'd all had months and months to deal with, and I was still drowning in.

"No one would let me through the gate to talk to them. I would have told them, but it wasn't necessary in the end," Jamie said, his tone somber.

There was a heavy silence that fell over the group, interrupted by Tucker's "charming" mouth. "Who's Mace?"

No one spoke for a few beats, leaving it to me to explain what I'd just as soon never talk about. "Charles Mace was my brother who I'd just found out about when I went to Undraland for the first time with Jens last year. My parents left him with Alrik when my mom was banished from Undraland. They thought it would be safer for him than to live as exiles in a world teeming with vindictive Huldras."

"They weren't wrong," Jens commented under his breath.

"Anyway, he was a pretty strong Huldra they'd collared to keep any chance of him whistling under control."

"A male Huldra? He could control people with his whistle?" Tucker had his studious face on – eyebrows knit together, arms crossed over his chest and no hint of sex jokes in sight. It was hard to recognize him without the sex jokes. "I've never heard of such a thing."

I shrugged. "What can I say? We're a weird family. We got his collar off and he helped us a lot. Helped tear down the Elvage portal, which is how he and I got thrown into prison there." I hated every word that came out of my mouth. I'd been silent for so long, and my words were now being used to cut me in my sore spot. I didn't want to talk about Mace. I didn't want to think about it or remember the awfulness. I wanted my brothers back.

Linus. I have to get to Linus.

I took a deep breath, my arms banded around my stomach to keep my guts from falling out all over the floor.

"Mace revealed himself as a practicing Huldra to the guards, and he told them he controlled me into destroying the portal, which is how I was let go with apologies and an escort by the Elvage Head of the Guard."

Jens grumbled under his breath, "That's not why you got an escort. Kristoffer wants to jump your bones."

Tucker shook his head. "But they'd have checked your hands and eyes and seen that he hadn't controlled you. How'd you get around that?"

I wanted to answer. Actually, that's not true. I wanted to run away from the question. I wanted to take a car ride to Nøkken and bust Linus out of the ground so anything could feel right again. My mouth opened and closed several times before Jamie took pity on me and answered.

Jamie cleared his throat. "She wouldn't let Charles take the blame for the portal and wouldn't agree to tell them he'd controlled her. She was set on dying with him. Charles wouldn't have that. He used his last moments to whistle her into forgetting who he was. Then he confessed his crime to the guard. He was beheaded straightaway. Lucy and I forgot all about him until the sirens jolted it all loose." He sat straight next to Britta, his arm around the back of her chair. "You'll have to excuse us; it's still quite fresh for Lucy and me."

Tucker was thunderstruck. "That's a terrible story. You're no longer in charge of nursery rhymes." He shook his head. "Wait. You only just remembered everything in the sirens' lair? It's been more than half a year since you came back to the Other Side, right? How's that possible? Huldra whistles usually wear off in a few hours or days."

Jens fielded this one, which was good, since my guts felt like they were hemorrhaging out of my body. "Lucy was more susceptible to him, and Mace had abilities like I'd never seen, apart from his mom." He laced his fingers together and placed them over his messy hair. "He was Hilda the Powerful's son. Bound to be some punch behind his blows."

The more questions Tucker asked, the worse the knife dug into my tender stomach. "What about this Linus bloke? Is he like Mace, then? What are we getting into when we resurrect him?"

Jens cracked his neck – a horrible rippling grind that made me cringe. "Linus had a tail, but it was removed at birth. Lucy was born without one. They don't have any abilities at all. I'm guessing Linus probably has a wall like Lucy's in his mind, with Hilda keeping his powers tucked away for the greater good. It's not safe for the public to have a Huldra that powerful unleashed on the world."

I kept my eyes trained on the tabletop. "Mom said a byproduct of her spirit inside me was my blonde hair."

Britta turned her head toward me. "Linus is sort of blond, too." She was a good friend to remember that. Jens had shown her a few pictures of Linus he'd taken on his phone. "Darker than Lucy's hair, but still not Undran."

I nodded, putting the obvious puzzle together. "Then I

guess you're right about Linus having her spirit inside him, keeping his abilities tucked away from use."

Tucker's gaze stared at the top of my head and trailed down to the tips of my hair that desperately needed a trim. "That explains how we got a blonde Undran with no abilities whatsoever."

I was tired of talking. I wanted my brother. "Jamie has to come with me to get Linus, but no one else needs to go. I want you all to come if you can, but I get it. Britt, Foss and Tuck don't even know Linus. It's just a little trip to Nøkken, and we'll be back before you know it with Linus 2.0. Easy-peasy."

"You know I'm going. I'm your Tom, and Linus was my friend." Jens pounded his fist twice on the table – not in an angry way, but to signify that he was in.

Jamie sighed. "Of course I'm going, but if we could make it a short trip, that would be preferable. I don't relish the idea of my child being born in Undraland with my father so greedy for his throne, and set that I should not be a part of it."

Britta was quiet, but firm as she spoke. "I'll not be going."

Jamie was the only one surprised at this news. "You're not? Surely you've forgiven me for how I acted when I was drugged by Jeneve!"

Britta softened, her hand resting on Jamie's. "I've put that out of my mind forever, since it wasn't you. I know you, Jamie, and I don't hold any of that against you or Lucy.

I'm not going because I'm pregnant. It's several weeks' trek to Nøkken and back, which will be a far longer journey if I'm there. If Johannes is bent on murdering you, I won't let him near our child. I can hide here and wait for you to return."

Of course I wanted Britta with me everywhere I went, but girlfriend was in the beginning of her second trimester. Ain't no way we were going to let her hike through the mountains and sleep on the ground.

"Then I can't go, Lucy," Jamie ruled. "Linus can wait until after the baby's born."

30

BASEBALL BATS AND FIRE

I stood so quickly, my chair toppled backwards. I glared at Jamie, leaning my fists on the table. *You will not take this away from me! Every day that goes by is a day someone might discover his remains! I've been without my other half for too long! I've let you escape your curse by coming into my dreams. I've done everything I can to make sure you can be with Britta without our bond getting in the way! You owe me, Tonttu!* I slapped the table in my fury, glaring at him with my upper lip curled in a sneer.

Jamie slowly stood, taking his time to tower over me and give me the full effect of his older-than-me status. *You will not throw your kindness in my face as leverage. What you're asking is much, syster. You had nineteen years with your brother. I will not miss a day of my child's life!*

Would that I could breathe fire. *Nineteen years? Nineteen years?! You try being a twin! You try losing every person in your family, then getting a new brother only to lose him a few months later! You lose everything you love, and then tell me what you wouldn't do to get one of them back! I don't care if I give us an aneurism! I'm going to get my brother, and I'm leaving tomorrow – with or without you!*

Jamie growled aloud. *You don't get to make decisions for the both of us just because you're the bigger child!*

I let out an audible screech of indignation and rounded the table to pound on him.

Jens stood, intervening in our silent feud. "Okay, okay. Why don't you two try talking out loud so the rest of us can help? It's getting a little intense."

I yelled, not caring how unbalanced I sounded, and pointed at Jamie. "He's trying to keep me from Linus! He doesn't want to leave Britta, so he's saying I shouldn't need to get Linus back now. That I should wait until after the baby's born. He's cracked, I'm telling you! I'll wait out the night here, but I'm gone by morning! My brother's rotting away in Nøkken as we speak! Linus needs me, and I need him!" I pounded my fist to my chest, my voice breaking without my permission. "I can't live like this anymore! I need my brother!"

Jens nodded, his voice even as he looked up at Jamie. "You won't leave Britta now, which I totally understand. You want to wait until after the baby's born, right?"

Jamie's arms flew out as he spoke. "Yes! She's being unreasonable! It might not even be real, what she thinks Hilda told her. I didn't hear a word of it!"

"That's because you were dying while I was being electrocuted!" I screamed, lunging at Jamie.

Of all people, Tucker intercepted my ill-intentioned advance, his hands up in defense as he positioned himself between Jamie and me. "Not that you could actually do any damage, being the pixie you are, but I'm his *vakt*. Best not attack while I'm in the room."

"I'm not crazy! I'm not! My mom told me where to find Linus, and I'm going! You can't stop me! You all were impressed with the farlig fisk and the Circhos? Wait till you see the depths I'd stoop to for Linus! Don't you *dare* try to keep me away from him!"

Jens remained levelheaded, and I couldn't decide if I was impressed by that or annoyed that he wasn't as furious with Jamie as I was. "Okay, Jamie. You won't leave your pregnant wife. When will you leave the newborn baby to go get Linus with us? When the baby's a week old? A month?"

Jamie shrank. "I can't leave a newborn. Give me a few months, at least."

Foss scoffed at this. "You're soft. You wouldn't be able to leave your child, no matter how old."

"How many months?" Jens asked his best friend. "Every month you're asking Lucy to wait is a month you're letting Linus die. You can only ask Lucy to be patient for so long." He addressed the room as if I wasn't there. "You all don't know. You haven't seen them like I have. They're the same person sometimes. The lengths they go to for each other?" He pressed his mouth to the flat of his hand and spoke into the flesh. "Lucy got pushed around by some girl at a school in Detroit when she was a teenager. Linus didn't even need to hear what happened. He saw her with a bruise on her arm, felt their freaky twin bond and beat in the girl's car windows with a baseball bat. Poured sugar in the gas tank, too."

Jamie didn't soften. "All that tells me is I don't need to hurry to get him out and about."

Jens wasn't finished, though I wished he was. "One of the soccer teams Linus played on in high school had a tradition of some mild hazing. Just defacing the newbies' jerseys. I can't remember what Linus's said."

"Skeleton boy," I choked out. "He'd lost a lot of weight and didn't want to tell them he had leukemia. We were new to that school, and wanted a fresh start. He was afraid they'd kick him off the team, or worse, keep him on out of pity." I closed my eyes, taking a step back from Tucker. "Don't tell this story, Jens. It's not relevant. I didn't hurt anybody. It was just payback for their prank."

Jens ignored my plea. "Lucy went into the locker room during practice, broke into every upperclassman's locker, stole their backpacks and game jerseys and set them on fire in the coach's office on his desk."

Foss, Tucker, Jamie and Britta stared at me with that opened-mouth wary look you'd give Charles Manson if he showed up in your church group asking for communion. Tucker took a step back, reevaluating me with a hint of that icky flirtation that made me want to give him a solid Scarlet O'Hara slap across the face. "Not such a pixie after all. Who knew you had that much fire in you?" He had the gall to wink at me.

My reply came through gritted teeth. "Keep. Your. Herpes. Away. From. Me."

"Stellar find, Jens," Tucker complimented his friend. "Fight and a fair face mixed with a little fire play. My favorite flavor."

"Control your man!" I glared at my boyfriend, who was building his own doghouse. "Thanks for that, Jens. Really. Thanks. That was a private story I didn't even know you knew about. You're not helping my case. I'm not going to set anything on fire here. That's Tucker's job. I only need you and Jamie to come with me."

Jens remained unshaken. "I said all that to tell you guys that you have no idea how far Lucy and Linus'll go for each other. The smallest offense gets capital punishment. Trying to keep her away from her brother? It's cruel, Jamie. You're being cruel, and I won't stand for it."

My mouth fell open as I began to draw a superhero emblem on Jens's chest and envisioned him with a cape flying out behind the collar of his black t-shirt. My heart swelled at the sight of a man who knew my brand of crazy so well, and still had the stones to defend me without blinking.

Jamie's jaw clenched, and I listened to him sift through different acerbic responses before he landed on something more congenial. "Be that as it may, taking me from my wife, whom you kept me from while she's pregnant, is also cruel. I've missed almost the entire first half of her pregnancy."

Foss had been silent for too long; I should've guessed something was brewing. "I'll be staying behind here. I'll help you prep for the journey and do whatever you need, but I'm staying on this side."

My head whipped around to stare at his closed-off expression. "What?"

"You can't really be that surprised. I'm dead in Undraland. If I come back, Olaf will have his men gunning for me. I'll be actually dead, and I've grown to like your world, stupid as it is."

I wanted to talk to him, to plead for him to come with me. His strength was invaluable, but I couldn't give him reasons to follow me to the ends of the earth or Undraland anymore. That would be my true cruelty shining through. I would stoop to whatever needed to be done to secure Linus by my side, but I couldn't string Foss along for the cause. "That's fair. Do you need any money for the ranch while I'll be gone?"

Foss didn't like me mentioning the loan I'd given him to start his business, but I didn't much care. I needed to be sure he was taken care of before I left. "I'll be fine. Ryan's been running things without me for a while, and we're still turning a profit, so I can start paying you back soon."

I waved my hand to brush away his comment. "I'm not

fussed about that. Just look after yourself while we're gone."

Foss nodded once, looking like a cowboy. "Will do."

Jamie huffed. "I'm sorry, Lucy. I won't leave my wife for anything. I've already missed too much."

Britta, beautiful Britta stood next to her husband, rubbing the small swell of her midsection. "Then I'll go with you. I won't go through the mountains, but I'll go through Elvage and wait there for you all to return. I won't have to hike through the mountains or go through Nøkken. It'll be a shorter separation. Does that work for everyone?"

Jamie closed his eyes, angry at me for Britta finding a way around his stalwart position. "What about my father?"

Britta flipped her braid over her shoulder. "When we pass through the gate to Undraland, we'll be in Elvage, not Tonttu. You and I should stay invisible as long as we can." She looked over at me with nothing but kindness in her eyes, despite the long trek I was putting her through. "Lucy wouldn't need to be invisible, though. Not really. Elvage doesn't communicate much with Tonttu, so by the time word reaches that Jamie's in Undraland, we'll be back at the Other Side, hopefully with Linus, whom I very much look forward to meeting."

I shoved past Tucker and wrapped my arms around my best girlfriend. "Thank you. I love you so much, Britt. I needed that. Thank you. Thank you. I owe you so much."

Britta smiled into my hair. "You owe me nothing. If I

were in the same boat, there's nothing I wouldn't do for my brother."

Jens met his sister's eyes with a gaze full of years of love and meaning. They'd lost their parents, and then Britta had been given no choice when her brother left for the Other Side. It was a deep and lasting bond they shared. Britta loved Jens, plain and simple.

With everything in me, I resolved in my heart that Linus would come back to me. That though I'd changed, and the world changed, we would get our same-old back. I would joke, and Linus would laugh. He would pick up his baseball bat when needed, and I would make use of my lighter and a little gasoline if anything ever came between us again.

31

WALKING AWAY

"I've already been through the checklist five times. I've got everything I need. Could we just go already?" I had burned through the last of my patience when Foss had asked me again if I had enough food for the journey. It was like the moment we stepped over the threshold to his expansive ranch, he felt the need to harp on me about every little thing. Jens had already stashed enough food in his red bag for ten of us, when only five were going.

"Jens is loading up the car. Maybe you could calm down a little. I mean, I don't really care, because you'll only be annoying me for a few more hours until I drop you at the gate, but for the sake of the others, you know, shut up. You're likely to find yourself gagged and thrown in the trunk if you don't give us all some peace from your mouth."

I glared at my former husband. "If I haven't said so before, your attempt at humor is your least sexy quality."

"I wasn't joking." Foss picked up Britta's backpack and Jamie's, slinging them over his shoulder as he walked to the door. "Do you have enough water in your canteen?"

"Sheesh! Yes, I remembered water, Foss." As soon as he exited to help Jens finish loading the car, I tiptoed to the sink and filled the canteen I actually *had* forgotten to fill.

Jamie and Britta came out of the backroom of Foss's giant brick and wood ranch holding hands. "Are you ready to introduce me to Linus?" Britta asked with a delighted smile on her freshly-washed face.

"More than ready. He'll love you guys." I touched the vial on the necklace I wore like a talisman of hope long forgotten and only recently rekindled. "Two weeks to get to Nøkken, and I'll have my brother back." It was worse than waiting for Christmas. It was worse than being dressed up for Halloween, only to have our parents tell us that we couldn't go trick-or-treating until dusk. It was waiting for my other half to return to me. A promise of winning the lottery if only I could hold out on a smile and a prayer for another couple weeks.

"What's Halloween?" Jamie asked, picking a mental image of me dressed as Harry Potter and Linus dressed as the grim reaper (Linus had a bleak sense of humor). Jamie hadn't exactly been ignoring me since it was decided we would go back to Undraland to find Linus, but he hadn't gone out of his way to engage in conversation. Something told me Britta had a hand in bringing him out of his funk and forgiving me partially for making his pregnant wife return to the land that had been so cruel to us.

I produced a grin for my laplanded buddy. "Halloween is October 31. It's a night when kids all over dress up in fun or scary costumes and go from house to house for candy. We say 'trick-or-treat', and the neighbors give you a piece of candy. You go through the whole neighborhood and end up with a sack of awesome to last you till Christmas."

Jamie and Britta looked at me with skeptical expressions, and then at each other as they burst out in laughter. "That's the strangest thing I ever heard!" Jamie exclaimed.

Britta's laugh since she'd gotten pregnant was loud and had a deep cackle to it that made me giggle every time. "You almost had us there, *syster*. Kids dressing in costumes to beg for candy like street urchins. Can you imagine?"

I opened my mouth to defend children everywhere, but Jens beat me to it when he reentered the kitchen after finishing up with the car. "It's true. Strange, but true. Lucy and Linus had the market on the holiday, though. When they got old enough to go out without Rolf, they stashed a spare costume in their candy sacks. When they finished their first round of the neighborhood, they changed their costumes and did a whole other round."

I nodded. "Two Halloweens in one go."

Jens let out an amused chuckle as he bumped his hip to mine. "Linus told me about the year you guys did the double Halloween, and then told your parents you were spending the night at a friend's so you could go down the road to the rich neighborhood and double-Halloween them, too."

I bumped his hip in response, unable to hold back my smile of pride. "That's right. I didn't know you knew about that. That was well before you came to work with us. Never underestimate what a girl won't do for a candy bar. Those country club houses gave out the good stuff. King-sized grand prize all the way."

He raised an eyebrow to go with his sexy smile, and I knew he was thinking about kissing me. "You're a conniving little vixen."

"Best thing I've been called all day." I nipped his lower lip.

Tucker breezed through the kitchen, grabbing an apple from the fridge and munching on it, his suspenders hanging at the sides of his pressed navy fitted pants. His tailored shirt fit his lean and muscular body like a glove, making him look almost handsome, if his sleazy personality weren't factored in. Despite the fact that we'd let him live when there really wasn't all that much a reason to, Tucker remained ever himself – the guy you warn all your girlfriends to stay away from, but they somehow never listen. "Morning, all. What a great day to go to a magical world and resurrect the dead."

I excused myself from the kitchen and waited out the others getting ready in the living room. Two days. It had taken two whole days of driving back to the ranch,

discussing too many things that didn't seem all that important when compared with the fact that my brother was
waiting for me.

When we all piled into the SUV, Jens relinquished his
driver's seat to Foss, who was bent on being argumentative
to mask his sadness at us leaving him behind. I actually got
to sit with my boyfriend in the backseat of the car, his arm
around my shoulders and me snuggled into his side. He
turned us invisible so we could indulge in a tame makeout
without making the other people in the car uncomfortable. My curls hung loose at my shoulders, and Jens
tangled his fingers in them as my lips parted for his. He
was torn between being gentle and ravishing my mouth
with his, so he vacillated back and forth enough to drive
me wild. I was still on the mend, but I had my fire back
with the renewed purpose I now held in my heart like a
torch. Jens loved me best when I was the most me, and I
hadn't been me in a long time. Every step I took toward
sanity, he cherished, and I knew with each kiss that I'd
been a fool to look anywhere but to him when I wanted a
mess of butterflies swarming around in my stomach.

The seven-hour drive felt like half an hour, but
somehow also like a week. No matter how close we got to
our goal, I wouldn't exhale until I saw Linus mocking me
for worrying so much. We'd had to make a pit stop at the
Huldras, so Elsa could give the modification on my eyes a
boost, in case Mace's magic had worn off and I couldn't
handle the Undraland sun.

Foss parked the car in the lot of the creepy abandoned carnival I told myself I'd never have to see again. The mood turned from anticipation to somber at having to split up our group that had grown to be our own family. Our family was filled with dysfunction and just enough love to justify a face-to-face goodbye from each member.

Foss avoided me, shaking hands with the others and wishing them a successful journey. Though I could tell Jens didn't want to grant me the privacy I needed to say goodbye to Foss, he did so anyway, waving the others toward the gate.

My gloved hands were shoved in my pockets, and when I spoke to him, I addressed his chest, not his eyes. We were far enough back from the ticket booth that his features couldn't be seen. "So, we'll be back in a month, month and a half."

Foss nodded. "You and whatever passes for your family can stay at the ranch until you get back on your feet. Your house isn't exactly livable." He paused, and then the wall between us began to show signs of cracks in the spackle. "I know you're mad at me for not going, but I actually have a business to run. I've been gone long enough."

I shrugged. "I'm not mad. You don't owe me anything. I was surprised, sure, but it's fine. I understand. I'll be back before you know it."

His tone was so sad, it made me look up into his dark eyes. "No, you won't. Whatever the sirens did to you changed you. The part of you that belonged to me is the one they killed. I see the way you look at Jens now. You'll come back here, but the you I wanted is gone for good. It's why I can't go with you. I have to move on."

I swallowed, knowing that he was right. I felt different now. I'd grown, not giving myself over to temptation when it presented itself in the form of a tall, dark and handsome man with a smoldering gaze hot enough to set a woman's panties on fire. "That's fair. For what it's worth, I'm sorry I let it all get so convoluted."

He rolled his eyes, as if I'd said something immature just to jab at his composure. "Of all the things I want, for you to be sorry is not one of them. I don't need you to regret me. I don't regret having you."

I despised all his mentions of various types of holding ownership over me, but I let that one slide for the sake of the adult moment we were sharing. "Then what do you want?"

"I want to be able to walk away. I want to walk away, and I want you to let me."

I nodded twice, mulling this over. "Are we still friends?"

He rubbed the nape of his neck. "Sure. Of course. Hey, we were married. If you need anything, I'm here. But I have to... you know, let you be happy with Jens. I won't try to pull you in two so much anymore."

There weren't words, so I bobbed my head, hoping I didn't fall apart in the parking lot, of all places. "Okay."

He pulled off his ruby ring and retrieved a leather lace from his pocket. "Over there you were my wife. This will help you, should you need anything. Use my accounts for whatever. Buy yourself something pretty and pretend I was thoughtful enough to get it for you." His fingers brushed my neck as I lifted my hair for him to have better access to fasten the knot.

I offered up a light chuckle, eyeing the ring he secured around my neck. "Thanks. I'll be sure to buy myself that pink unicorn I always wanted."

He tapped his heart as he faced me, expressing things we wouldn't say aloud. "I'll be here when you come home."

His use of the word "home" tugged at my heart. I had no place to rest my head, but he was offering me his. Not just me, but a place for my brother and Jens, the man who managed to edge out the hold Foss had on me. He loved me in the way a man should love his wife – enough to do what was best for me, even if it hurt him.

I touched my heart and then butted the crown of my head to his sternum. "Go be happy."

His fingers shifted through my curls, and I felt his nose bury itself in my hair. Foss inhaled deeply, and my heart hurt for the tenderness I could not return. He released me and picked up my hand, pressing his lips to the center of my palm with his eyes closed. When he dropped my hand, I felt my heart banging in my chest. "This is me walking away," he said, his voice gravelly. He traced his thumb across my lips, and a million emotions swirled up in me like too much dirty laundry shoved into an already over-burdened machine. His lips brushed mine in a closed-mouth farewell that jerked me around with its beauty and finality. When he whispered against my lips, I could feel our hearts breaking in unison. "And this is you letting me. I'll see you soon. Goodbye, lovely wife."

"Goodbye, darling husband." I meant to say the words, but my heart could only commit to a whisper, for fear of my voice cracking under the pressure we put on each other to be more than either of us could handle.

When I turned around, Jens was waiting at the plexiglass window where I'd first met Mattie. That's the thing about a man you don't deserve, but wish you did. He doesn't complain when you make him wait.

I trotted over to the group, the light purple heels of my Chucks dragging on the asphalt. My hands were shoved in my pockets, and I'm sure I looked as low as I felt. Jens enveloped me in his warm sugar cookie smell, and instantly, I was home. My travelling home that never left for good, and was always there for me to return to when I wandered. "You alright?" he asked.

I nodded into his black t-shirt. "You're too good for me. I'm sorry for putting you through all that. It's over now, but you didn't deserve any of it."

He invisibled us so he could kiss me. It was a simple, tender blessing that communicated more than what needed to be said. When we reappeared to the group, our hands were linked, and would remain that way. Jens bumped my hip with his. "Let's go, Mox."

32

MATTIE'S WARNING

Mattie was not there this time around. Jens frowned at the change. Instead of the graying pudgy woman who loved to flirt with Jens, there was an official-looking man who looked like he had a yard-stick up his shirt to make him sit so straight. Jens flashed his gold badge, and the man signed us in for what felt like half an hour. Then he finally waved us through the turnstile.

"I don't like that," Jens commented under his breath, reaching for his knife out of habit when anything made him uneasy. "Mattie's never not here on a Tuesday."

I shrugged. "She's not allowed to take a sick day?"

"Something feels off. Stay close."

The slow and broken organ music piped through the loudspeakers, adding more unease to the group as we walked quietly through the empty park.

Tucker wore a frown uncharacteristic of his jovial nature. "I haven't been home in decades. Is it always this tense? What's wrong, Jens?" He touched his left suspender in anticipation of a fight.

Jens glanced over his shoulder toward the entrance, where the man who checked us in was murmuring into a walkie-talkie. There was no one else around, so I couldn't imagine who he might be communicating with.

Something's wrong. You and Britt should go invisible, just to be safe. I voiced my fears to Jamie, and not three seconds after they disappeared, Jens turned invisible and grabbed onto Tucker and me. I looped my fingers onto the waist of Jens's jeans.

Tucker's arm wrapped around my shoulders like a human shield. Or actually, like an elf shield, if you want to get technical. He pulled me tight to his side as we moved slowly forward. Protecting me was every bit as effective as protecting Jamie, so I could only protest his close proximity in my head. He tugged on my hair, tilting my ear toward his mouth. "If I say so, I want you to run back through the gate. Get out of the park and phone your husband, *käresta*."

I frowned. "I won't leave you guys."

Tucker glanced down at me with a disapproving look. "Foss can bust us out if we're in a jam. You won't be leaving us. You'll be getting us help." He pressed his lips to my temple. "Jens is never paranoid. Be ready."

My heart thudded as we moved toward the house of

mirrors. The terrifying clowns painted on the walls of the attractions added to the goose bumps on the back of my neck. The hair on my arms stood at attention, which sealed the deal that we were walking into something dangerous. *Jamie? Maybe this isn't safe for Britta. If Jens is worried over nothing, we can always come back in a minute and get her. If we're walking into a trap or something...*

I heard Jamie whisper to his wife to go back with Foss. She had her phone on her and the ability to stay invisible, so she silently dropped behind and made her way back out the gate. *I won't let her be harmed. Tell me she'll be safe with Foss. Tell me my baby will live.*

Jamie, I'm sure everything's fine.

No sooner had I uttered that thought did I hear Mattie's pinched voice ring out through the park. "Run, Jens! It's Johannes!" I turned my head toward the front gate and saw Mattie seemingly pop into view from out of nowhere as she broke free from a suddenly visible man's grip. The Tomten pulled out his knife and dealt with his victim the only way Undraland knew how.

There was a scream, a slice, and a gurgling. Red poured from Mattie's plump neck like poorly made paint that dripped when you smeared it on drywall. Her knitted orange cardigan began to mutate to a violent shade of maroon, her spectacles falling to the ground seconds before she did.

Tucker's hand went over my mouth, but he didn't need to muffle any sound. I couldn't bring even a squeak through my throat, so choked was I at seeing the older woman brutally slaughtered because she cared for Jens.

The man who checked us in was yelling in our general direction, signaling for his men to snatch us. Out of the attractions that had seemed empty came Tomten soldiers with their swords drawn. We were invisible, which was our only advantage. Dozens of men closed ranks across the gate, moving as a wall of one toward us, and doing a slow sweep of the area so as not to miss their prey.

Over the loudspeaker boomed a man's authoritative voice. I cringed as the sound mingled with the clunky clownish organ music. "Prince Jamie, your presence is requested in your father's palace."

Me? They want me and not Jens? Why would father send the guard to fetch me if I was already coming through the gate?

I answered Jamie's unspoken question with the thing he didn't want to say to himself. *Jeneve tried to kill you and make it look like an accident. I don't think your dad's as concerned with appearances anymore. He wants you dead, Jamie. We have to get out of here.*

How? We can't go back the way we came. The only way out is forward, through Undraland.

Jens hesitated, seeming to think the same thing. He reached out and pulled Jamie closer, and without the need for words, Tucker moved from Jens to Jamie without being seen. Now we each had our guards, but we didn't feel safer. Tucker kept one hand on me and one on Jamie, linking the four of us so we could see each other. His grip on my waist was tense, his calculating stare sizing up too many things for me to keep track of.

I was acutely aware that there were likely more guards that were invisible, following closer than I was comfortable with. We were being corralled to Undraland, though I couldn't figure out why.

Through the door to the maze of mirrors.

Through the mirrors to the door in back.

Through the door with the razor-toothed clown painted on it.

Into Undraland, or more specifically, Elvage.

Smack in the middle of a battalion of Tonttu soldiers with their weapons at the ready. "Seize the prince!" the leader shouted.

I touched Linus around my neck, whispering a prayer for my brother to forgive me for coming so close, and yet still being so far.

Love the book? Leave a review!

Don't stop now!
Read Book Eight in the
Undraland Series, Lucy at Last.

ABOUT THE AUTHOR

USA Today bestselling author Mary E. Twomey lives in Michigan with her three adorable children. She enjoys reading, writing, vegetarian cooking, and telling her children fantastic stories about wombats.

While she loves writing fantasy, dystopian, and paranormal tales for her readers, Mary also writes romance under the name Tuesday Embers, and cozy mysteries under the name Molly Maple.

Visit her online at www.maryetwomey.com, and sign up for her newsletter, so you never miss a new release.

www.ingramcontent.com/pod-product-compliance
Lightning Source LLC
Chambersburg PA
CBHW032009050726
47590CB00006B/2109